Santa Barbara Literary Journal

Volume 13

Mysterious Ways

May 2026

Editors

Maryanne Knight, Editor-in-Chief
Zachary Murdock, Poetry Editor
Frederick Williams, Fiction Editor
Calla Gold, Fiction Editor
Junior Bases, Assistant Editor

Featured Artist

Diana Salas-Deitch

Santa Barbara Literary Journal
Santa Barbara, CA, U.S.A.
www.santabarbaraliteraryjournal.org

Published by Noleta Press LLC
P.O. Box 1251
Goleta, CA 93116 U.S.A.

ISBN: 978-1-971404-00-4

Copyright © 2026

Mysterious Ways

May 2026

TABLE OF CONTENTS

LETTER FROM THE EDITOR

Maryanne Knight

Dear Reader,

Thank you for picking up Volume 13 of the *Santa Barbara Literary Journal, Mysterious Ways*, featuring poems and stories that bend the rules of reality as we think we know it to explore death, grief, security, expectations, and the power of music and the written word.

We're thrilled to showcase the work of artist Diana Salas-Deitch, whose watercolor explosion of color titled *Waterfall* graces our cover. I met Diana years ago through her spouse, writer Nicholas Deitch, who selected the art for volume 12. When that issue ended up with one final page that needed artwork, Nick asked Diana if she could sketch something for the space. She came through with art tailored to the story it followed.

I liked how Diana used the story as her springboard and asked if she'd be up for illustrating the whole next issue. I am deeply honored that she agreed and even more thrilled with the results. You can learn more about Diana and her creative process in her chat with Calla Gold on page 197.

This issue is the second collection from the call for submissions for Volume 12, *Superposition*, which brought an abundance of outstanding short fiction and poetry to our editors' desks. When it became apparent that we had more content that we wanted to print than we had pages to fill, we began planning the next issue, looking for common themes in the submissions to distinguish the two volumes from each other. Here, you'll meet characters with unusual abilities and perspectives, from Olinda's writing to Sal and Antonio's music to Theo's psychic bond with history, with a touch of whimsey in even the most serious pieces. I hope you find the stories and poems as compelling as we did.

I'm grateful to all the writers and poets who stuck with us and kept their work available for consideration in our current issue. I'm also grateful to our editorial team, Poetry Editor Zachary Murdock, and Fiction Editors Calla Gold and Fred Williams, who evaluated everything that came in and made recommendations for both volumes. I also want to thank the newest member of our team, Assistant Editor Junior Bases, for his help putting this issue together. Junior is expanding our online content by interviewing writers, poets, and artists for our online blog. We're also building out our archive of fiction, poetry, and art from both the current and prior issues. Check it out at SantaBarbaraLiteraryJournal.org.

Lastly, you may have noticed a new logo on the back as the Journal has a new publisher, Noleta Press. We're excited to continue delivering the same high-quality content readers have come to expect from the *Santa Barbara Literary Journal*. We hope you enjoy this collection as much as we enjoyed putting it together.

Warmly,
Maryanne Knight
Editor-in-Chief

May 2026

The Girl Who Wrote the Storm
by Diana Salas-Deitch

10

THE GIRL WHO
WROTE THE STORM

by Calla Gold

Olinda set the gather basket down, dirt escaping through gaps in its rush bottom. Beans lay clean over layers of bitter radishes, beets, and rock roots, the source of the stubborn clumps of dirt. She sank into the chair, pulling her bad leg across the thigh of her good one to pry off the boot. Rubbing her twisted foot, she focused on the fluttering pea vine flowers out the window and the shadowed forest beyond. She'd come so close to being caught straying from the cottage.

Gran kissed the top of Olinda's head. "So dear a one."

"Stop filling her ears with your nonsense. She's brought more muck than gleanings for all her scrabbling about." Her grandah's gruff, scratchy voice sounded disapproving even when he asked someone to pass the parsnip mash.

Olinda stared at the clean-swept floor and the crumbles of dirt between door and table. She was beyond wishing for his praise. Her chest heated, tight, bursting to share her tidings.

She would bide. In a short turning of the glass, her grandah slammed the wooden door, and soon the sound of an ax splitting logs drew forth from her a long sigh.

"He'll be after that for a bit." Gran laid aside her bone needles and the blanket squares she was knitting for the coming winter. Her gray-blue eyes met Olinda's. "You're fair twitching lass. What mischief have you?"

"I wrote the story from your wish," Olinda whispered. "The grinding wheel once again turns. How be it made true?"

"You speak of the old mill?"

"Aye. It grinds again."

Gran covered her mouth and turned away. "Oh, Lass, I set you so many tests and we've uncovered your gift at last."

"My gift?"

"Your letters. You wrote my wish for fine ground wheat for a proper loaf. It came to pass. Olinda, you are a truth writer." A tear fell from Gran's eye. "Words you scribe, may come to pass, Goddess willing."

Olinda shook her head. "Grandah said I wasn't worth the price of a lame old carthorse."

"Your grandah sides with the King's witless folly and his crusade against hedge witches, magic, and the old ways. He values only coin and the desecration of all I hold dear. He would abide not to suffer a witch at his hearth."

"The hedge witches, charm makers, and keepers of the old ways are all women. Does the King send his soldiers through his kingdom to kill women?" Olinda's hand covered her mouth.

"Aye. That is why we hide our lessons."

"This is most dire," said Olinda.

"Aye, lass, that is why your miracle is a message from the Goddess."

"Pray, tell me why."

"The prophecy, lass. 'A champion will appear when the need is nigh.' Our King's bloody war rages. His soldiers would steal our sons, plunder our stores, and burn our huts for the sin of displaying a wreath of dried herbs, runes painted upon a doorpost, or singing an old chant to calm a baby. All for the profit of dust and sorrow." Gran squeezed her eyes shut and took a deep breath. "The very air I smell these past days is tainted with the smoke of death. Our people bide in this far valley, holding no royal favor."

"I wager, the King's men could not find us here. And I'm no gift; with this foot, I'd be first caught."

"Olinda, attend—the gift of the unseen courses through our line. Your mother was fearful, and my only chance, until you," Gran said. "Clamp tight your tongue of this boon. Scratching of the quill is not for such as we."

"I scribed a miracle?"

"Aye, lass."

Olinda dropped her head into her hands, hiding the joy writ upon her face.

***

The next dawning pinked the sky. Olinda stared at the water cascading and tumbling unevenly from the wooden buckets on the water wheel, half hidden by the leaning millhouse above. Grinding stones rattled and boomed from within the gristmill, alive with the changing of seed to flour.

Amid the splashing bright drops flung into the air, Olinda picked out the scents of hay, pig grease, and corn powder. The voice of the miller's daughter calling her brother to wind the wheel tighter filtered through cracks in the ancient timbers. Whitewater chuckled and churned beneath the wheel, nudging branches, leaves, and chunks of blackened dirt and algae to the creek edge.

Climbing slowly to dampen her limp, Olinda crested the hill. Curling russet hair loosened from her braid as the wind gusted wavelets across the mill pond. Ducks gathered, diving and feeding just beyond the still canvas of water where the current stilled the chop. The serene water's reflection painted the scene, capturing the white spruce crowding near the shore with fleecy clouds above. The tranquil water's path narrowed, sucking noisily into an overgrown reedy bank. Long unturned, the waterwheel screeched and groaned. Olinda pressed her hands to her cheeks.

I felt no magic yesterday, she thought. Yet her foot ached as if stepped on by a tinker's pony.

***

Back in the cottage, Olinda complained to her Gran of the grievous pain in her foot after writing the tale of the mill.

"Scribe your words beneath the arch of two or more trees," Gran said. "Thereby, the magic collects."

"But Grandah forbade me to enter the forest last spring."

"The forest is where the magic lives. That's why your grandah spends his days cutting down the tallest and straightest of trees. He cares not whether the butcher has a roof over his house to protect his family. He seeks to blunt the touch of the other world."

"And profit from the sale of felled wood?" Olinda asked.

Gran nodded. Her sparse white hair was stiff as the coat of the parson's terrier.

"'Tis the bent limbs of a gnarled tree," Gran murmured, "in union with another that weathers the storm. Seek the Goddess' arbor when next you venture to scribe a tale."

14

***

The following day, Olinda slipped from the hut, limping past the straight and tall trees. High upon a mountain flank, bordered by great boulders, she found two majestic oaks, just as Gran described. Scrambling under the jagged curvature of their joined branches, she sagged against a firm trunk. In the valley below sat Gran's cottage, the horses and cows grazing, and villagers carrying baskets and water sacks to congregate by the well.

Crushed moss, sweet rotting bark, and pungent pinkbells filled her nose. She lay her tired body back, the motion of the earth beneath her as true as the patched clouds marching above.

Sitting up, she scribed the words, "The cloud rose like a leaping horse." She gazed at the sky. Sluggish clouds moved until one fell and another rose. A nervous laugh escaped. She crafted a new story. "A lone scout, in King's colors, rode ever nearer their high-up, hidden valley, turning away from a steep crest to explore elsewhere."

She hadn't smelled the hint of death on the wind like her gran. Yet she trusted the nose that could scent deceit, lies, and the reek of stolen belongings. Olinda's hand stilled. Her eyelids drooped, and the sun-warmed breeze drifted, lifting fine wisps of hair from her cheek. She let go the birdsong and leaf rustle, and slept.

Her resting place was mirrored in a palette of deathly gray. Birds huddled in silence, claws gripping branches, a fox darted into its den. Olinda crept to the ridgeline on hands and knees, high above the arching oaks. Peeking over the edge from the cover of a thorny thicket, the cliff fell away and took the air from her lungs.

The valley below was a tangled wilderness, deterring most

travelers, but not the King's scouts. Their encampment, set in an old course of the meandering river, was six tents strong. Two soldiers sparred, swords glinting in the late afternoon sun. One of the swordsmen tilted his head back, eyes aimed at her hidden aerie. She saw his cruel face as close as a tinker by the cottage gate.

She jerked awake. Color and brightness made her squint. Was the dream a disproof of her tale? A warning? "Goddess, pray tell me, do I dream? Do you visit me truth?" A dizzy thickness gripped her head. A gusting, chill wind whipped the faint scrape of crossing swords to her ears. Her head cleared. Speaking aloud, she said, "A new tale must I write. Goddess, keep me." Olinda's hand curled over her heart.

She leaned her back against the rumpled tree trunk, eyes following the leafy boughs above. Limbs danced and dipped forward to braid into the arms of their mate.

The scritch of her quill unfurled the tale of a gentle breeze that twisted into a cruel wind. With brief words, the wind blew a terrible storm toward the thicketed valley beyond, making the tethered horses pull, neigh, and break their ropes. She wrote their manes tangled, catching low branches, galloping opposite their inner compass for home. Her letters sent them seeking strange pastures in lands with scents untested, three moons from where they last grazed. An ache pressed on her twisted foot. "It's not enough," she shouted into the rising wind.

Groaning and panting as she pressed on, she described twisting, dark clouds, bunching like frightened sheep over the valley. They gathered and split apart to spear the land with lightning, thunder, and a deluge that rivaled the breaching of an earthen dam.

The relentless fury of the storm crackled and boomed.

Olinda's skin contracted, gooseflesh hard. The shelter of the trees couldn't shield her from the wrath of the tempest. Her twisted foot swelled against its boot.

As if touched by the Goddess's care, she grasped the pull of sapping strength, the lack of vigor to climb down home. Chilled fingers pressed the point of her quill. She saw in her mind's eye the choked valley's river. Its many tributaries gushing forth, water shooting upward when blocked, uprooting trees, boulders, and brush.

Like a swooping bat, she could see the undulating folds up-canyon. Deep ravines overwhelmed by torrents of rain, laid bare as brush was ripped away as easily as lace from a collar. The low rumble of boulders colliding in the river sent vibrations deep into the earth. A stand of trees inundated by the flood stopped a crosswise log, then another. Boulders wedged next, smaller rocks filled the gaps, and brush shot up to the top like a haphazard thatched roof. The frothing tide reared and churned. A sideways waterfall roared against the cliff face to thunder into the ancient riverbed under the cliff. Gushing down canyon, the river pushed a heaving mound of brush, logs, and giant fists of stone. The six tents and the King's men were scoured from the shelf at the cliff's base.

Olinda shivered, soaked to her skin. The sky above, dazzling then dark, rendered the scraping of her quill an unseen act. Paper torn, ink long gone. "A black horse escaped the home pasture and galloped to the girl on the mountain," she wrote, a sob escaping unheard. Her numb fingers, no longer able to grip the quill, shoved it into her sack. Paper bits ripped away into the shrieking wind.

Night descended. The pound and beat of pouring rain turned for a moment to a thousand tiny whip cracks of sleet.

Olinda's arms squeezed her spindly legs for warmth. Unseen knots and jagged bark bits jabbed her back as she bent herself into the hollow in the oak's trunk. Ten paces away, a limb crashed to the ground, its sodden heaviness drumming through the earth, rattling her teeth.

The howling gale lessened with the sharp crack of nearby twigs. A snuffling breath, meadow grass sweet, warmed her forehead, and the tickle of muzzle whiskers scraped her cheek.

"You came." Unable to climb the back of the tall horse, Olinda limped in the dark, one hand clinging to the knotted mane, the other outstretched. The howling wind hid all but the snap of breaking limbs. Olinda's scalp constricted against the sting of freezing rain, while rivulets worked their way under her collar. She wished she'd written a saddle.

An obstacle bulked darker ahead. Her outstretched hand bumped into the bark of a downed giant spruce. Short, broken branches offered up their rungs to aid her climb. The scratchy forelock and bony nose nudged her as she clambered up off the sodden ground. Lightning turned night to day, the horse, a carven statue. Olinda worked her stiffened legs across his broad, wet back. She pressed her nose into his thick, bristling mane, inhaling sunbaked pasture dust where rain failed its onslaught. Her frigid fingers threaded together underneath his neck, gripping tight as he plunged down or slid sideways in the mud of eroded washes. Branches poked, chafed, and snapped over her back.

In three turnings of the glass, muddy, miserable, and wearied, she slid to the ground by the garden gate with a splash of boots, then bottom. She sat, wet to her sagging belt, teeth chattering, and brushed the black horsehair from her woolens. Sucking hoof steps retreated along the lane toward the pasture,

1 8

dissolving into the whistling wind.

The gate creaked as she scraped it open, calling her Gran. Grandah, hair wild, silhouetted in the doorway, stumbled forward, grabbed her arm, and dragged her into the cottage. Slamming the door shut against the wind, he yanked her into the light of the fire. Muddy water flowed off her, meandering between the cobbles of the hearth and creeping onto the plank floor.

He pushed Gran away as she rushed toward Olinda with arms outstretched.

"I forbade her the forest," Grandah roared, glaring at Gran. "Do you see the twigs in her hair, the mud upon her boots, the blue at her lips? She's near dead." He shook Olinda by her arm and pointed his bony finger at Gran's chest. "It is your nurturing of folly that makes her think a lame, young girl can wander safe in the wickedness of the forest." His scowl focused on the muddy tracks while Olinda's head sagged.

"I crave your forgiveness, Grandah," Olinda said in a quavering voice, bowing her head. She looked up at Gran and gave her a secret smile.

"Leave us, old man. We have heard enough." Gran pushed him back and pulled Olinda into a protective embrace.

"Foolish girl." He swatted the air above her head, dislodging a small branch. He stomped away, muttering.

Gran led her close to the fire, her silent fingers stroking warmth and love into stiff muscles. Under the cover of a blanket, Gran pulled Olinda's arms into dry clothes and pushed a bowl of warm stew into her cold hands.

Olinda whispered to Gran of seeing the King's men in the near valley, her scribed story, the Goddess's dream, and how she wrote the storm. From the other side of the room, Grandah growled, "You coddle that child like an orphaned goat. Only she gives no milk." He left them with a huff, a stomp, and thumped up the wooden steps to the loft.

In a low voice, Gran said, "That wasn't your first storm."

"No?"

"You conjured its twin the night you near died being birthed. That's how I knew you had the magic."

"Did I conjure my foot atwist?" Olinda frowned, trying to massage away the pain.

"Lament not that frailty, child, for it makes you obscure to those who seek a magic's root. Aye, and let it remind you, there is a toll for every enchantment."

***

On the next market day, Olinda led the donkey toward the well. She'd packed eggs, butter, and wooden bowls. Ahead, a tinker shouted from his oversized cart. "The King's arrows I did find, two saddles, and an unstrung bow. What'll you trade me for this fine camp kettle of the King's? I warrant you, it softens the oldest mutton and flavors the meanest of shriveled roots for the wayfaring traveler."

"Where from, old man?" shouted one of the villagers.

"Down below at the turning where the river runs wide. There be logs aplenty. Might make meself a cabin."

As she passed the wagon, a neighbor haggled over a water-stained saddle. Olinda couldn't stop the smile from pulling up her cheeks.

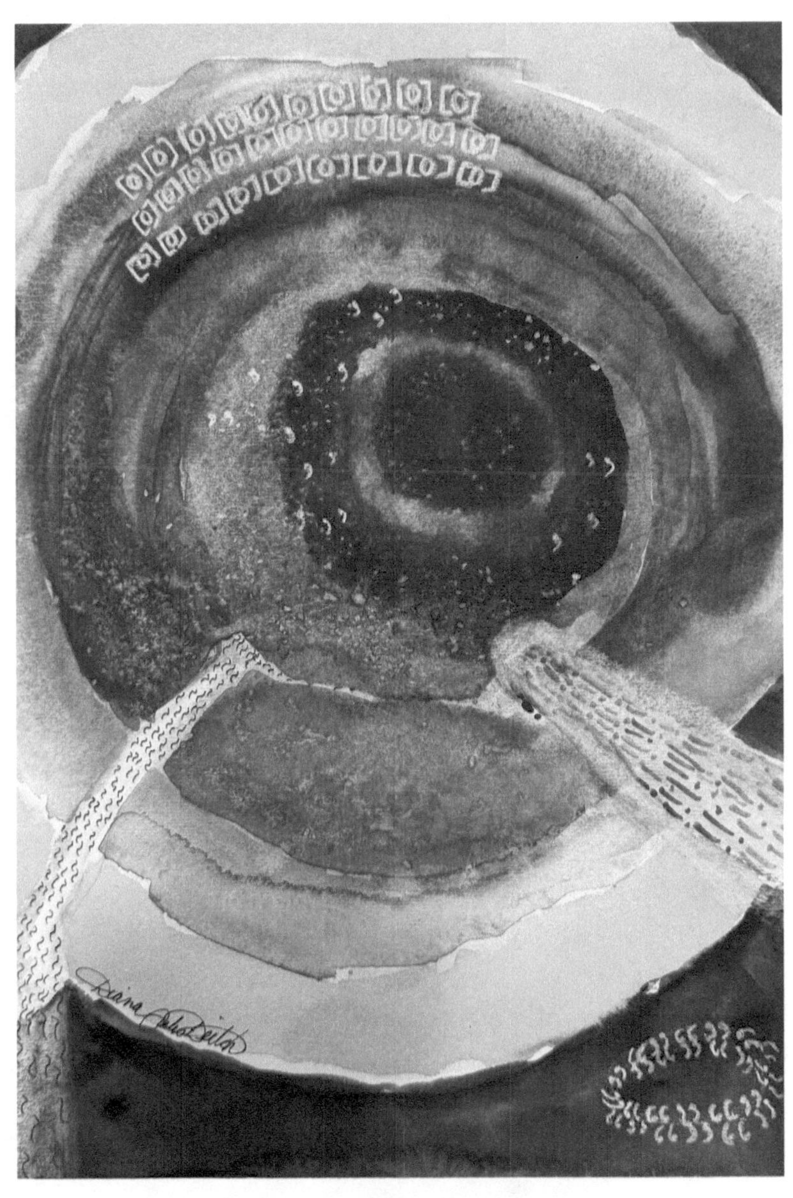

World Makers
by Diana Salas-Deitch

WORLD MAKERS

by Caitlin Swalec

Inspired by the line "Words are world-makers" from Robert
Macfarlane's Underland

If words are world makers,

spaces must be the expanse between celestial bodies.

A sentence is the solar system,

galaxies contained within each paragraph.

""	satellites and moons
~	an asteroid belt
,	a star
!	a comet
;:...	constellations
'	interstellar dust
[()]	layers of the atmosphere
<u>C</u>	Capital is the sun and
.	the boundary of our cosmos

If words are world makers,

grammar and syntax create order.

Inflection is visible light,

traveling cosmic distances from lips to ears.

FONT measures three dimensions,

speech becomes the fourth.

We breathe in punctuated pauses
to prove oxygen exists.
These words support life forces.

It's beautiful to think that your grandmother's
        handwriting,
holds the characteristics of space,
her history, your familiarity, a specific gravity.

If words are world makers,
each language forms a parallel universe.
Galaxy, *galaxia, galaxie, Galaxis,* галактика,
        Gökada, 星系,

المجرة
Infinite iterations existing on one page.

Thoughts left unsaid are black holes,
dangerous, enigmatic, rebellious, nebulous.
Speak carefully.

If words are world makers,
I could believe in a god,
as long as I can fill my mouth with:
onomatopoeia, harmony, kaleidoscope,
aurora, petrichor, sequoia.

If words are world makers,
What do you call
(home)?

I FILL MY PAIL

by Wendy Jean MacLean

At the beach I fill my pail
with metaphors and beautiful words
and virtuous intentions.
The pail shapes them into walls of sand
crenelated with shells and small stones.
A glorious creation.

Again and again I fill my pail
and empty it, letting the hopes
shape towers, letting the images emerge
from clumps of wet sand.

At the end of the day
someone will gleefully smash the castle
as they walk the beach.
If any walls are left, the rain
will flatten them. Tomorrow
I am free to begin again
if I choose.

But I am tired of filling my bucket.
My hands are weary
from digging and dumping.

For years I have been defined
by the incessant building and destroying
of castles and paragraphs,
towers, and proposals.
If I leave the castles, but bring the pail,
will I find myself repeating
the same folly of indignation and imagination
stuck together with sand and pride?

I write these words knowing
that the rain will come in the night
and wash them away, yet again.
Tomorrow I will find new words
for hope and parapets.
A glorious creation.

Affliction and Revelation
by Diana Salas-Deitch

AFFLICTION AND REVELATION

by Shira Musicant

I found Ma's left leg half buried in the backyard. Like it was trying to dig down to China. I brought it in.

Dad slammed down his beer can, punctuating his words. "Jesus goddam straight," he said. "So that's where it went to."

Dad and I had been on the leg look-out for nearly an hour, though I was doing most of the looking.

Ma, being the Bible expert in our family, chided Dad, "Lord's name, Buzz—watch how you use it." Then me, "Sonny Boy, don't you do like your dad."

"I knew I could find it, Ma." I hefted it back to her. I helped out as much as I could. This was a few months before I saw my helpin' weren't helpin'.

Ma hadn't always been losing herself but started in on it once she took up with her Bible. Or maybe she took up with her Bible when she'd started in on losing things. Usually not as consequential as a leg. Just toes or earlobes or something small. I'd go looking for her and find her in the bedroom where she'd be dropping parts before my eyes, her missing pinkie lying quiet under her bed, listening to her read Proverbs.

Dad used to say, "You know the Lord, boy. If He'd wanted your ma to stay whole, He wouldn't a made her come apart so easy."

"Though our outer self is wasting away, our inner self is being renewed day by day." That was Ma—always reminding us of the bigger picture.

Dad's outer self didn't exactly come apart, but his things drifted away. I had to search for his keys or his drink. Or both. His job left soon after. "Just up and walked away," he said.

Dad's job on the run, I had to get some work. "Idle hands," Ma reminded us, looking for her own. I found them on the kitchen counter behind the toaster, not really hiding, just tucking away. Must've tired while making a sandwich or thinking 'bout dinner.

I got a job at the grocery after school, bagging and stocking, while Dad snoozed through the day. "Not idle at all," he said holding up a mixed one or a beer. He showed his other hand and picked up the remote.

"This life," Ma said, holding tight to her own shoulders, "ain't nothing but a light momentary affliction." She must've had Corinthians memorized.

Being gone all day at school and then at the grocery, I couldn't keep things tethered. The house started in on falling apart. Cupboard doors unhinged themselves, springs sprung through upholstery, and spoons went missing—a neighbor brought three of them back that he'd found in his garage.

Window screens slid off the windows and rested on the floor, refusing to return to duty.

One day my own right foot skedaddled off my leg. Took off, heading out the front door.

"Well, I'll be a rat's ass," Dad said, slamming down his beer, as he watched the foot saunter off the porch. He had his own way with words. "I think it's 'scaping, Sonny Boy. You go catch it, then rustle us up some chow."

That was when I knew I had to go. I figured there was a place somewhere in the world where people didn't go falling into pieces, a place with no drifting or dropping or losing. There had to be. I was gonna find it. I packed some clothes and a bologna sandwich in a paper bag and picked up the Bible Ma had given me. Then I put it down.

Dad sputtered awake when I patted his shoulder, looked at my bag then back at me.

"It's time, eh Sonny-Boy?" He said it like he knew I was always gonna leave afore I started in on coming to pieces myself. It was almost too late. He coughed and wheezed. "Come back and see your old Da someday, okay? Mix me a strong one before you go. Get on now."

I peeked in her bedroom and saw that Ma was quoting scripture to a room full of her parts. "God will wipe away every tear." She was knee-deep in Revelation.

I closed her door and walked out of the house. The moon came out big and round that night, like Ma's old serving platter, like Ma serving up the moon. Darn if it didn't light up the road.

CONCLUSIONS

by Christopher Buckley

Life is a whim of several billion cells to be you for a while.

                                                    —*Groucho Marx*

We're sitting in our thin bones, our thin skins
which also are just portions of dust. Clouds swirl
on the horizon, the image of our cerebellums
as we try to recall our green and limber days,
our once acrobatic brains, what someone tagged
our "salad days," which did not mean the summit
of our talents, but bread and vegetables, the little
we could afford.

                         5 years since I've seen my compadre
who's driven the length of California to sit on the patio
recalling that deck over the Pacific, the grad-school rental
we swore was built of driftwood— afternoons and
evenings with tumblers of cheap, seed-green wine on ice
to help us toss our boneheaded lines and 1/2 thought-
    through
ideas over the railing, into waves.

                                         Time and distance—
this is likely our last visit vertical on the planet...
thing is, despite the express of years, the mind-wrenching
catholic schools we both survived, he's shifted

to Shintoism, which no more believes in a tilt-a-whirl
of angels in the clouds than hell or heaven, and
from all I've read, and for different reasons, I agree.
In short, we believe only in what we remember.
Neither of us thinks we're coming back to do
anything quite as wondrously vainglorious again,
despite Tarot readers, mediums, or orthodoxies
designed to put off fear of nothing else at all...
from which science says we emerged, no more than
a coincidence of cosmic quarks... and now all
we're left with is a long-shot hunch—were we,
just lucky, nothing, but a few lucky, residual sparks?

for Gary Soto

THE SPIRIT CHILD
L'ENFANT SPIRITUEL

by Reed Venrick

She loved horses, she spoke
Softly to the mares, just as she did
With friends and children.

The officers' horses would strain
On tethered ropes to stand
Closer, nudging—stomping

Hooves, now and then, to ward
Off flies—but some soldiers
Complained. Jeanne knew

More names of horses than
She did of men. She, born
In a limbo land of war and religion,

She, frightened by fire, not because
Of heat, she said, but smoky
Campfires caused her sinuses

To stop up, and then, the tone
Of her voice would drop into

A hoarse whisper. Jeanne didn't

Remember, but her mother said
A burning candle had fallen
On her when she was just three

Or four. The hot wax had left
A permanent stomach scar;
That must have been when her

Fear of fire began. Once,
Jeanne overheard her mother
Speaking covertly to her older

Sister, Jeanne's favorite aunt.
"When I saw the mark the wax made—
"Where did it burn?"
"Her umbilical cord."
"So what was the—"
"Then I knew."
"Knew what?"
"I shouldn't say.
"Then why speak of it?"
"Because I saw it in a dream."
"A dream?"
"A nightmare."

Jeanne of Arc came from the northeast
Of west Francia, near the Meuse
River. The mother had five children,

Jeanne was the fourth of five,
The others were brunette or
Blond, but Jeanne had dark

Hair she bobbed at puberty.
Her peasant father, when drunk,
Ranted that Jeanne was not

His blood, but her mother cried
And vehemently denied. And
He could be violent—he'd struck

The neighbor, who suggested
Jeanne was a witch—hadn't they
Heard the stories about voices

She'd heard? And as Jeanne's
Mother watched her grow, she
Would gaze at the child that

Soon she called her "spirit child."
Sometimes the mother would
Smile with delight, as a parent

Will, but sometimes she went
To weep in the kitchen, and
When the sister came in to ask

What was wrong, Jeanne's
Mother would shake her head,
And when the siblings asked why

She referred to Jeanne as "her
Spirit child," she would only say
It was the same night Jeanne

Was born that it was revealed, but
The older sister rebuked the mother—
"You shouldn't call her that."

"What?"
"A spirit child."
"And why not?
"Sometimes words make things come true."

Kept
by Diana Salas-Deitch

KEPT

by Alyson MacInnis

She didn't remember the path here. Not fully.

Just the way the wind shifted when she stepped through the narrow cut in the hills, and how the canyon walls leaned in like they had something to say—if only she'd be still long enough to hear it.

The dog moved ahead without needing to be told. White, silent, steady. Her ears flicked back occasionally, listening for the woman's pace, but she didn't look behind. She already knew the way.

Ashara followed slowly, her boots crunching dry dust, the canyon cool and dappled with the kind of light that lives in places untouched by sun. She wasn't sure why she had come—not exactly—but her chest had felt tight for days, and something inside her had begun to press outward, like a bloom forming beneath the skin.

Now here she was.
And it was quiet enough to feel the shape of herself.

The stone walls on either side bore shallow carvings—
spirals, long lines, curves like waves, some barely visible. She
hadn't noticed them the first time. Or maybe she hadn't let
herself look.

She paused when she saw the first mark she recognized.

A spiral. Not the kind that opens.
The kind that draws inward.

She reached out without thinking and ran her fingers along
the groove.
Cool.
Clean.

Beneath it, a word. Faint. Almost erased.

Kept.

She touched it again, slower this time.

Not a message.
Not a warning.

Just a reminder.

She had come through this place once before—

and left something behind.

The dog whined gently ahead, just once, then settled at the base of the canyon wall. Her eyes tracked Ashara's movement. She was waiting now.

Ashara moved forward.

There it was.

The mark she hadn't meant to find, but had come for all the same.

A handprint, small and worn. Fit almost perfectly into a carved line that looped twice before anchoring into the rock.

Her own palm hovered over it.

She didn't remember pressing it here.
But her body did.

Without ceremony, she placed her hand into the stone.

And the canyon answered.

Not in words.
Not in light.

But in feeling.

A presence rose—cool and ancient, but not strange. It

moved through her arm, her chest, and settled low behind her ribs. Something she had laid down long ago. Something not ready then.

Now, it stirred.

Not as a weight.
As a return.

And the canyon held her.
Not with arms,
but with knowing.

Ashara stepped back from the wall, slowly.
She flexed her hand once, then let it fall to her side.

The canyon held no echo.
But everything in her felt quieter now.
Less scattered.
Less waiting.

She looked to the dog, who had settled into a sphinx-like pose at the base of the wall.
Calm. Watchful.
Eyes half-lidded, as if she too felt what had passed.

Ashara sat down on a low stone ledge and let the silence press close. Not heavy—just full.
The way the air feels after someone speaks the truth aloud for the first time.

4 0

Her breath moved easier now.

She touched her chest, just beneath the ribs, where the return had landed.
It didn't pulse like the seed she still carried.
It didn't glow or speak.

It just was.

A part of her again.

Not reclaimed.
Rejoined.

Something she had left here on purpose, when she couldn't carry it through what came next.
Not because it was bad.
Because it was hers.

Too raw.
Too wild.
Too whole.

And now, she was strong enough to hold it again.

The dog rested her chin on her paws and exhaled.

Ashara closed her eyes.
Let the stillness deepen.
Let the return settle.

She didn't think of names.
Didn't ask what it meant.

She just let it be there.

Like water returning to water.
Like a vow kept so quietly it was never broken.

When she opened her eyes again, the light had shifted.
The canyon's shade had cooled further, and the sound of running water was clearer now—steady, sure, the kind of stream that doesn't rush but endures.

The dog was already standing.
Not pacing.
Just ready.

Ashara stood too. Her legs felt rooted, not heavy.

She didn't look back at the handprint.

There was no need.

What had been left there was no longer waiting.

She walked in silence.
Not toward anything.
Not away.

Just with.

The canyon narrowed, and she followed it.

The path dipped toward the sound of the water, where moss lined the rock and willow leaves quivered against the light. A small bird called once, sharp and clear.

She paused at the bend, where the trail slipped out of sight again.

And before taking the next step, she placed one hand against her chest.

There it was.

Not glowing.
Not moving.

Just a truth returned to its keeper.

Kept.

THE VOID, OF COURSE

by Valerie Girard

I face the dawn's glimmer,
Cloudless luminations peek over the distant ridge.
They bid me,
Settle now, in reverie.

My coffee steams its essence
Into the morning's chill,
A stop to gather guidance
As I often will.
This moment, an emptiness warbles.
Clanging for attention.
I surrender to its call.

Then:
Something emerges, silently,
Unraveling my pact with Time,
Even as bird and brook transmit
Their secret code, a call to drop into the unseeable.

I inhale the dusty scent of autumn, then whisper,
Come to me, Mystery, weave through me
Your hallowed tendrils of the Unknown.

I exhale, empty, open, receive,
As I long for the moment's reveal.

There.

It's the Void, the Void of course, the Doer's nemesis.
With this, all thoughts cease.
A portal opens. An invitation to drop to Nothingness,
To view its event horizon and acquiesce
To its undoing into no-thing.

I surrender, then receive this offering,
Mystery's song, so subtle.

> *The Void, of course, is yours to stream.*
> *Empty now, into Nothing's dream.*
> *There's Nothing to know and nothing to see,*
> *Free your Self through the Mystery,*
> *It's all within, as Me and thee,*
> *And now, take rest and Nothing be.*

In the Great Silence, then,
Nothing is,
A sanctuary of becoming.

by Diana Salas-Deitch

I'LL TAKE YOU THERE

by Terry Sanville

Sal clutched his tattered jacket around himself, its tabloid lining fluttering in the frigid Chicago wind. He moved slowly through the snow, turned down the first alley he came to, and leaned against the brick building. Sirens echoed in the distance, but otherwise he was alone in the night, temperature dropping. He blew on his numb fingers but it didn't help; his hands felt like lifeless stumps.

The sky had cleared and the moon shone full. Sal pushed his way through the wet snow with warehouses on both sides. He looked for that mistakenly unlocked door and the promise of an inside refuge. An empty dumpster or some kind of shed would also do. He'd been stumbling along for blocks, maybe for hours, after the folks at the rescue mission kicked him out for being drunk and causing a ruckus. They had called the police.

Near the end of the alley where it emptied out onto the side street he found a set of service doors. He tried the knob, using both hands. It turned. Sal stopped to listen. All quiet. He pushed one side inward. It opened, but only a little way before running into something metal and unmovable. He shoved his knapsack through the narrow opening, knelt and turned sideways, then wiggled and squeezed inside, his breath coming in great heaves, spots appearing before his eyes.

He landed on a hard concrete floor. He shut the door quietly. A metal security bar across the service entrance had kept it from opening all the way. His breath lightly steamed in the air, but it felt much warmer being out of the wind. His hands, face, and feet regained feeling; the tingling and lightning-strike nerve pain made him groan. He flexed his hands and shoved them under his armpits for further warmth.

Finally, he stood and rummaged in his knapsack for the small flashlight that he'd lifted from a 7-Eleven along with a pack of batteries. The Korean owner had chased him down the street, yelling *"dodung, dodung!"* Sal had easily outrun the old man, although his back and legs had ached for hours afterward.

The flashlight's beam illuminated a large high-ceilinged room filled with three-tiered racks packed with crates and boxes, and aisles wide enough to accommodate a forklift. A freight elevator occupied a space next to the service entrance that Sal had just squeezed through. Open stairs led upward.

Sal climbed to the warehouse's second level. It felt warmer and had no window openings to the outside. He continued to climb, stepping slowly without making noise, but a faint sound made him halt and hold his breath. Someone close by tuned a guitar, taking their time at it since the strings must have been new and not stretched yet. He retreated to the second level and followed the sound to a walled-off room against the building's far side. Its door was closed but a light shone brightly from under it. An enormous padlock, like the ones used in old railroad yards, hung unlocked from its hasp.

Sal opened the door a couple of inches and peered inside.

"I hear you. What do you want?" The man's voice accosting Sal sounded much larger than its source.

"Nothing, just someplace out of the wind," Sal answered.

A smallish brown man with dreadlocks sat cross-legged against a far wall, cradling a guitar in his lap. Sal pushed open the door and entered.

"Close the damn door. Someone might see the light."

"You'd better put something under it. I could see light from the other side of the building."

"Shit."

The guitar player rose and searched the room, which held racks of musical instruments in their cases. Finding an old rug, he jammed it under the entry door and returned to his tuning. Warm air flowed in from a wall vent.

"Why are you here?" Sal asked.

"Probably for the same reasons you are. I got fired from my day job and lost my apartment. I missed one fucking month's rent and they kicked me out."

"You got any food?" Sal asked. "I haven't eaten for a day or so."

"No...and I just finished my bottle of Night Train, so don't ask."

"Shit."

"Yeah, I tried lifting some grub from a supermarket down a ways. But their security was on me like white on rice."

Sal grinned. "Hell, I can't even walk into one of those places anymore without some jerk following me around. My name's Sal, by the way."

"Yeah, well you look like Che Guevara. All you need is a

beret. I'm Antonio."

Sal looked around the room and discovered it stored more than musical instruments. On a middle shelf, the barrels of assault rifles and machine pistols peeked out. Other shelves held stacks of laptops, iPads, assorted computer equipment and big-screen TVs. Another held jewelry boxes containing who knows what.

"What is this place?" Sal asked.

"If I had to guess, it's a fence's storeroom."

"Yeah, but so many musical instruments?"

Antonio grinned. "Whoever ripped this stuff off knew what they were doing and had good taste. All the guitars are high-end collector models – easily a couple hundred grand worth sitting in those cases."

Sal removed his knapsack and jacket and sat with his back to the wall not far from Antonio. "Don't worry, man. I'm not a violent person, just cold and hungry."

"That can make somebody desperate. But hey, it's winter in Chicago. You can't be too smart if you're wandering around outside."

"Yeah, so how did you get in here?"

"Rolled a dumpster under the fire escape, climbed to the roof and worked my way in through a ceiling vent."

"But the lock on this room's door looks pretty ugly."

Antonio chuckled. "These hands are good for more than playing guitar."

"So you think you can play, huh?"

Sal had pawned his own guitar three months before, his last possession of any value, part of his long slow slide into drifterdom after the divorce when his wife took everything, including his dignity and a future.

Antonio stared at him for a minute. "Yeah, I play guitar for a living. But the clubs and cafés in Chicago want something that I can't give 'em."

"So why'd you pick that guitar? It's a classical. Nobody listens to that stuff."

"Shows how much you don't know. This isn't a classical guitar, it's a flamenco guitar, an old Manuel Ramirez."

"What's the difference? They look the same to me."

"A classical guitar has a thicker neck, higher action and a warmer sound. Flamenco guitars have a thinner neck, lower action and a brighter, more punchy sound."

"Huh. Who knew?"

Antonio grinned. "Me."

The old man seemed satisfied with the tuning and played simple slow chords. Then he began more intricate fingerings, slow at first, filling the room with sounds as dark and rich as a good California cabernet. The tempo increased, and his fingers plucked arpeggios faster than anything Sal could manage. Sal closed his eyes, shuddered one last time, and breathed in the warming night air. The warehouse's musty stench of cardboard, old dirt and rat turds had been replaced with scents from unfiltered cigarettes, strong coffee, spicy foods, and the hint of a woman's perfume.

Sal opened his eyes and gazed around him. "What's going on?" he muttered.

Antonio continued to play, intent on hitting all the right notes with just the right attack, the right vibrato, the right feeling. But instead of sitting cross-legged on a concrete floor in a musty storeroom, he perched on a stool, on a small stage, in the corner of some sort of café crowded with couples at rustic wooden tables and men at the bar, most speaking Spanish.

Plates of partially eaten tapas littered the table where Sal sat. His hunger had vanished. He wrapped his hand around a short tumbler filled with vino and downed it in one tilt.

An old woman, with iron-gray hair and built like the trunk of an ancient oak, got up to dance. Two more joined her. They moved with authority, with determination, yet with mature grace, accenting the guitar's rhythm with the stamp of their low-heeled leather shoes. Antonio ended the music with a flourish and the applause rang loud in the low-ceilinged room. Sal reached for the half-empty bottle of wine before him. But in an instant it dissolved into thin air. He had returned to the storeroom and its hard concrete floor.

"What the living hell was that?" Sal asked Antonio.

"That was one of my own compositions. I've been working on it for a long time."

"Yes, yes. But what was that—the café, the dancers, the wine?"

Antonio grinned. "So you too let your mind travel with the music and were taken to Spain and some backstreet café in Madrid."

"Was that just some kinda mind trip? An illusion? But how—"

"It doesn't happen all the time and I can't control it. But when the music is just right..."

"Huh."

"So, do you play guitar?" Antonio asked. "I saw you watching me closely and figured you did."

"I mostly play jazz and blues, electric blues. But I also like the old delta styles."

Antonio pointed. "Pick a guitar and let's hear you play."

"Damn, you're a hard act to follow."

"Hey, it's just us players here. No pressure."

"Yeah, right."

Sal went down the rack full of guitar cases, checking the tag on each that noted the make and model of the instrument. He pulled a small hard-shell case with a faded "fragile" sticker pasted to it from the rack and laid it on the floor. Inside, a beat-to-hell rare National tri-cone resonator guitar with its chrome finish almost worn off stared back at him. Hauling the heavy instrument into his lap, he tuned the strings then checked the case's storage compartment and retrieved a brass slide.

Sal stared at Antonio and grinned. "I figure, slide blues is about as far from flamenco as you can get—no possible comparison."

"You'd be surprised. Just play, will ya? Take me south to some juke joint where the black folks have reasons to sing the blues."

Thank God for muscle memory, Sal thought. He inserted the brass slide over a pinky finger and began to play. At first his music sounded harsh, bouncing off the concrete. But then the bass notes kicked in and the rhythm made both of them jerk and move to the sounds. Sal closed his eyes and sang some of Robert Johnson's blues, and other down-home stuff, where the guitarist has to work hard to create a full sound to back up his or her singing, and to play something that folks could dance to.

Sal's fingers hurt from fretting the guitar's heavy-gauge steel strings. But he kept on. The storeroom slowly changed into the inside of a ramshackle joint, its walls a patchwork of weathered boards and rusted corrugated siding plastered with posters and beer signs of obscure brands. Old black men in field clothes along with some younger ones wearing WWII Army uniforms filled a rough plank bar. Couples clutched each other, women with their heads on their partners' shoulders, and danced to a slow tune that Sal found himself singing, something about a woman having left her man, on a night train, and how he tried in vain to forget her. Cigarette smoke mixed with weed, burning his eyes.

At a break between tunes, he reached forward and grabbed a glass filled with clear liquid resting at his feet and took a big gulp. It wasn't water, and he choked on the white lightning that seared his throat. Some of the crowd stared at him and laughed but they all clapped enthusiastically after he finished each tune. He sat in a corner along with a couple of other grinning dudes who clutched their guitar cases between their legs and waited their turn. Slowly, in flashes, the storeroom returned to its old eclectic self.

Antonio sat with his head back and eyes closed. "I can almost hear the trains, feel them as they rumble and sway through the night, passing through stations filled with nothing but ghosts."

"Yeah, the blues can take you there," Sal murmured and enjoyed the comforting quiet in the softly-heated storeroom.

"Do you suppose we'll ever return to that place where we're a part of it?" Antonio asked.

"I'm taking it one day at a time . . . and today's a good one. Tomorrow? Who the fuck knows?"

Antonio sat forward and pulled his guitar close. "Keep playing those blues in 'E.' I want to see how we might sound together, you know, a delta-flamenco fusion sound." He laughed as the duo tuned their guitars to be in the same pitch.

They played non-stop for some time, Antonio easily adapting to the pattern of chords laid down by Sal. They didn't speak, stared straight ahead and worked the sounds. Once again, the storeroom dissolved. A listening crowd of all ages surrounded them. Sal and Antonio stood in a subway station somewhere with their hats laid out on the platform and filled with greenbacks. But in a blink of time, they found themselves crouched at a tiny table, on a rocketing train, streaming past houses, farms, and cotton fields, precious light shining through windows that burned as bright as the sun, the warm forgiving sun.

***

"I asked you to come down, Mr. Lavine, just after I called the Fire Department."

"Thanks, Joseph. What made you call them?"

"When I came in to check your building, like I always do on Wednesdays, I found a whole bunch of dead rats, scattered everywhere. Before the fire guys showed up, I climbed to the second level. I found a storeroom unlocked. Someone musta broke in 'cause I checked that lock just last week. I had a hard time gettin' in 'cause they'd shoved a rug under the door."

"Slow down, Joseph. Who are you talking about?"

"The two dead guys inside the room."

"Dead guys? Holy hell, what were they doing in there?"

"Looks like they were playin' music. When I found them they were just sittin' there, frozen like, hands still wrapped around their guitars and big smiles on their faces."

"So what did the Fire Department say?"

"The Captain's still upstairs if you wanna talk with him. But he said he figured the building's old furnace had a cracked manifold and that it'd been leakin' carbon monoxide for days, maybe weeks. The poor bastards didn't have a chance."

The landlord shook his head and sighed. "Well...at least they were smiling."

WE SHOULD BE READING WILLIAM BLAKE

by William Doreski

At dusk the blue remainder
of the day spills into our hands,
freighting us with heavy matter.
Meanwhile the grief of rain

has flushed into our basement
where mockeries of sea serpents
breast the chop and deliver
frights and petty annoyances.

We should be reading William Blake
and balancing his illustrations
with the evidence of our lives.
Yes, we see his creatures fidget

at the edge of the flat Earth
we conspire to somehow inhabit.
Yes, we read his bearded gods
as distinctly as a child would,

cushioned by muscular nudity.
The fistfuls of blue sizzle
and scorch, but we can't drop them.
Not in this world although maybe

in Blake's, where John Milton
atones for his visions, and clouds
form pedestals sturdy enough
to bear every symptom of guilt.

Eight Bridges
by Diana Salas-Deitch

EIGHT BRIDGES

by Ted Olson

In a frenzied dance, the snow swirled, twisted, and spun in the glow of Craig Ladd's headlights. It was hypnotic, the way the flakes caught the light and sent it flurrying. It blurred the road. Craig moved his eyes—checking the guard rails, watching the curve in the white line near the shoulder, noticing the occasional spark of a posted reflector—to keep from being lulled into carelessness.

He'd made this Christmas Eve trip numerous times, from Hoback Junction to Bondurant and back. He knew each curve on the highway between the two Wyoming towns and could anticipate the required nudge or tug on his steering wheel the way a barrel racer knows when and where to shift her weight. The road followed the Hoback River, crossing it on eight bridges between Bondurant and his place a mile or two east of the junction.

He'd finished delivering a load of toys, donated clothes,

and boxes of pens, paper, markers, and books to the Church of St. Hubert the Hunter for the annual Bondurant Santa Extravaganza. This year, businesses, churches, and families throughout Sublette, Teton, and Lincoln counties had been especially generous. All wrapped in shiny Christmas paper, the gifts had filled seven jumbo-sized trash bags.

He'd rendezvoused with his friend and former brother-in-law, Stuart McAskill, at the church. They'd unloaded the gifts, unbagged them, and stacked some of them around the glowing tree in the church's sanctuary. What they couldn't fit near the tree, they put in Santa's Wheelbarrow for delivery later that evening. Then Craig vacuumed the carpet, Stuart set up extra chairs, while Shannon, Craig's sister-in-law and Stuart's ex-wife, worked down the hall in the kitchen taking cinnamon rolls out of the oven and glopping them with handfuls of creamy white frosting. Behind her, a silver pot of wassail sat on the stove, wafting apple cider, orange juice, and cinnamon, all getting along together in the air.

Stuart took the wheelbarrow and headed to the rector's office, where he decked himself out head to toe in red velour with white trim. He had a draping, dusty-white beard and mustache, but he was rail thin, so he used a foam-rubber, strap-on belly he'd bought from a theater company in Jackson and tied a down pillow around his backside. Once the soft red coat was on and buttoned, the cap fitted on his head with the white snowball dangling to the side, Stuart was transformed.

Cinnamon rolls and cups of wassail sat on serving trays, the lights were turned down, and Amy Grant's *I'll Be Home For Christmas* played on a boom box when the mayor and town council members finally arrived. Minutes later, kids and their parents came in. Craig watched for a while, then slipped out to the narrow hallway, put on his wool jacket, slapped some droplets from his Stormy Kromer cap, and pulled it onto his head. He started for the door. His truck sat in the parking lot next to Stuart's, already covered with snow.

"Hey, Craig, where you going?"

Shannon stood outside the sanctuary, her arms behind her back. She started toward him, untying the red-and-green apron around her waist.

"We're done, ain't we?" Craig adjusted his cap and reached for the door handle.

"Well, yeah. But they're just getting started. And Stuart's still gotta make his grand entrance." Shannon hung the apron over her arm. "You know he needs you there to take a few of his jabs. You two are a team." The arm holding the apron opened in a backhanded way, and the apron swayed beneath it. "C'mon back in. Relax."

Craig peered through a small window in the log-frame church. "Well, not sure I'm cut out for that role anymore."

"That's no way to talk, mister. You'll always be part of our family." She waved backward toward the rector's office. "Hell, Stu's still family, and we've been divorced three years now." She watched him, and the look in her eyes was so familiar it made him ache. "So you gonna stay?"

He looked out the window again. "It's gettin' thick out there."

"And what are you gonna do tonight, once you get home?"

He turned, taking in the colorful lights in the sanctuary, the mingling people, the flying bits of conversation, and the rippling laughter. "Start a fire in the fireplace, maybe," he said. "Have some coffee. Maybe some Dewars."

"What about tomorrow?"

"I got a cousin in Wilson. He's asked me over for dinner. Maybe I'll go."

"Well, listen…just a sec." Shannon raised her finger as if she would stop time with it. "Hold on. Don't go yet." She disappeared into the sanctuary and a moment later returned holding a giant cinnamon roll on a paper towel.

"I already had one, thanks."

"Have another one." Shannon held it out to him.

"I don't need—"

"Just take the damn thing." She pulled the paper towel corners over the roll, twisted them together, and set the bundle in his hand. "For the road."

Craig looked at her, scratched his eyebrow, and tried not to get too close. But he took the roll, and she patted his hand. It warmed his palm. He was near enough to Shannon to notice the necklace that draped over the collar of her turtleneck sweater, emeralds and rubies fashioned in the shape of holly leaves and outlined in gold. Even in the dim light, it glowed. It looked good on her, on that sweater. He turned back toward the door.

"I know how you're feeling," Shannon said. "It's been a tough six months for all of us. I'm feeling like a part of me's been stolen. You've been with someone your whole life, then they're gone outta thin air. It hurts. Hurts terrible. Mom's really struggling. She'd love to see you, ya know. We all would."

Craig stared out at his truck.

"Listen, you call us when you get home, okay? If you don't, we'll call you. And tomorrow, if it gets too much for you, come back out to the tavern. Stuart's closing the place, having the family over for drinks and dinner again, just like always. He didn't tell you?"

"It's not like I've been that accessible lately."

"Well, you know you're invited. Officially. Don't matter what time it is. You call or just come out. You got Stu's number?"

"Yep."

"C'mere." Shannon stepped forward and hugged him, but he kept his arms out, in part to keep the cinnamon roll from her hair. Even her hair felt familiar. "You be careful." She stepped back a bit and then said, "I guess, me being here doesn't help, does it."

"I didn't say that."

"You didn't have to."

"I gotta leave."

***

The roll sat on the passenger seat next to Craig's gloves and cell phone, and the cab brimmed with the odor of maple and cinnamon. Growling, Craig's gut laid claim to it. He might have eaten it then, but he figured he best keep his hands on the wheel.

His wife, Sharlene, and their two girls had always joined him on this jaunt. When they were younger, the girls had counted the bridges on the way back from Bondurant. In the back seat they would squeal a bit after bridge eight, knowing they would be home soon, and the gifts and the lights and the morning fire were only hours away. Once, the two got into a squabble about which bridge they'd crossed—six or seven. As the argument became piercing, Sharlene turned around.

"Hey, gals," she said. "Coming home, I've noticed that after we cross bridges one, three, five, and seven, the river flows on the left side of the road. After two, four, six, and eight—it's on the right side. So look—" She reached over and pointed out Craig's window, her finger in front of his nose. "The river's on the left, so we're between seven and eight." She nudged Craig.

"Wouldn't you say, babe?"

"Yep. You nailed it, Shar."

The girls settled down. During the rest of the drive, thinking that Craig and Sharlene couldn't hear their whispering, they planned to get up early the next morning, get the fire going, and have breakfast ready before their parents awoke. That was a great year.

But thanks to a drunk tourist from Florida in a rented car, they were gone. They were taken last spring. Craig had thought about staying home this Christmas. So much easier that way. Cutting the tree, weaving a giant pine wreath and hanging it on the barn, making clootie dumpling and rum sauce—things they'd all done together—seemed pointless. But Sharlene, her soul rooted in a long line of Scottish fastidiousness, had always been a stickler about tradition.

So come Christmas season, Craig started in, mostly for Sharlene's sake. But after finishing the lights on the house and the barn and the stables and the front fence, then staring at the glowing lines at dusk, he was still hollowed out. He wondered again if it all was worth it. And then in his head he saw his wife take her don't-mess-with-me stance, a hand in her back pocket and the other hand wagging a finger in the air. And in that instant, her voice had chimed through his thoughts. *You're just going through the motions, mister. You best put your steelies into it.*

Well, some kids will be happy. He remembered the frosting-covered faces of two boys he'd seen minutes before leaving the sanctuary. They'd taken a few silvery icicle strips from the tree, placed them on the tip of their tongues, and with puffed cheeks, blew air so the silver lines streamed in front of their faces. One held the strips to his nose, then inhaled so a couple went up one of his nostrils. Craig had looked up and found Shannon leaning against a wood pillar, watching the boys, too. She'd looked over and caught him, though he hadn't meant to stare.

Craig let that image tread water in his mind a bit, and for a moment, he wished he was already home.

At a curve in the highway, a moose calf darted up from the brush. Its hooves slipped, and its legs spread on the snow-packed road. The image of the two boys and Shannon in Craig's mind blew apart. He hit his brakes. The truck hit the calf and continued toward the embankment, and Craig saw only Sharlene sitting behind him on their four-wheeler and his two girls behind them in the plastic toboggan, laughing and sounding like birds.

His truck rolled several times before coming to rest, driver's side in the snow. His left shoulder hurt, and as he got his senses about him and unbuckled his seat belt, the pain spread until it was suddenly sharp, like a sledgehammer to his collarbone. His seat belt seemed to have held everything in place, because once he released it his shoulder fell to pieces. He tucked his left hand beneath his right arm and held it against his ribs, hoping to keep his broken shoulder from moving much.

Snow had burst through his window and left his face wet and cold. He smelled antifreeze. Hisses, pops, snaps, and sizzles seeped in from behind the dash like a backroom conversation. Small bits of his window lay sprinkled on his jacket and his door. His half of the windshield lay buried, a gray mass in front of him. Cracks spread across the windshield's passenger side, turning the snowy hillside into puzzle pieces. This sideways view made his head spin.

Through the broken passenger window above him, cold air settled into the cab. The glove box hung open, empty. His gloves, cap, cell phone, and cinnamon roll were gone.

His truck sat at a precarious angle, still tipped toward the incline, and a few yards farther, the Hoback River. If he could get his legs up onto the seat, he figured he could use the center console as a step and the passenger headrest as a handhold, then lift himself through the window and shuffle off the truck. He'd have to be careful about it. Any quick shift of his weight could send his truck tumbling again.

He twisted to move his legs between the steering wheel and the console, hugging his left arm to his chest, until he was able to get a knee on the console and pull himself up by the headrest. Reaching through the broken window, his hand found two plastic stumps where the side mirror had been. He grabbed one to steady himself and shifted both knees to the console, squatting for a second before standing. He could see his breath. His shoulder began to throb.

Behind him the river moved softly. The gurgling was more of a whisper, as if the water itself was keeping a secret. But he was close enough that the whispering sounded more like a threat.

His truck had cut a path down a steep grade about fifteen yards from the road. In that swath a few small pines were twisted and pressed, their thin trunks fractured. Looking at them, figuring what manner of leaps or steps he'd have to take, he saw the broken saplings as his route back to the highway.

He thrashed until one knee was up, through the window, and onto the door. He pulled his other leg through and would have crouched and jumped, but favoring his left side caused an imbalance he didn't consider. He stumbled forward, wheeled to his right, and was hardly able to push with his boot as he left the truck. His jaw hit the oil pan. He felt the hot exhaust pipe through his jeans. He landed on the snow, and a jab near his backside stopped him.

His truck turned slowly at first, but the weight shift carried the passenger side over, the tires moving up, then stopping skyward. The cab slid down on its roof and settled into the riverbank.

He lay there a moment, letting the snow rake across his newly lacerated jaw. It left a dark spot behind when he sat up. He wiped his face on his sleeve and stared down at the truck, its hood and cab nearly submerged.

He bit his lip.

He spotted one of the broken saplings above him and went for it, his free hand reaching and steadying as he churned upward through the snow. Amid all that movement, he swore he heard branches break behind him, but he wasn't about to turn and look. It was hand-in-snow, clawing and pulling. Feet lifting and stomping and scrambling and pushing. The grade became steeper as he climbed, until finally he saw an edge of ice and asphalt.

He stood on the road and for a moment the world seemed plumb straight again. Without looking back, he pressed his left arm inward, and began labored steps toward Hoback Junction.

Within a few yards, on the far side of the highway, lay the dark mass that he'd hit. He walked to it, hoping the calf had died instantly and chafing in his gut at the thought of having to put it out of its misery. It lay still and silent, and from the dark crescent running from its back to its belly, steam rose into the air and disappeared. Craig drew in a breath, and along with his shoulder, it made his chest ache. *I'm feeling like a part of me's been stolen...Mom's really struggling.*

He turned the collar of his jacket up around his neck. He thought he heard his cell phone go off. He thought he heard someone hollering. No recognizable voice, only a muffled shout, as if someone he couldn't see was trying to get his attention. Both sounds he knew were impossible. The silence was playing with him.

He slipped his hand into his pocket and continued walking, a step or two from the asphalt. It pissed him off that it took so long to make his way forward. In spring or summer, or even fall, the walk home would have been harmless. But winter had its way of exacting a toll. And on any other night there'd likely be traffic.

Of all the nights I could pick.

He missed the cinnamon roll. He wished he could at least smell it. He could smell nothing. The world's smells seemed to dry up in winter air. The best he could do was remember the sweetness of cinnamon, raisins, currants, and molasses as they came together in Sharlene's clootie dumpling. At first the memory buoyed him a bit, but he looked up at the stretch of road, seeing nothing but the straight white path that vanished to a point in the snow. He stepped but seemed not to move. Nothing changed.

The shivering started as brief bouts through his neck. He reached up and clumsily brushed snow from his collar, but it didn't end the shaking. He stepped faster and looked ahead, hoping to see a bend in the road, perhaps the glow of approaching headlights.

A gust blew suddenly from the other side, and the snow caught the air, revealing sailing tendrils, folding and curling across one another. They taunted him, for they seemed to hang too long in the air to be part of nature. It was weird the way they danced and circled above the road, as if showing off in front of him.

The road came to a bridge. Below him the mottled channel of black water was broken only by frosted tree branches or skeletal brush protruding from the bank. The river flowed to his right, so he figured he was probably at bridge six.

His steps slowed, or so it seemed, for it took forever to cross. The bridge looked as if it extended itself as he went, becoming longer just to annoy him.

After bridge six there was a house on a hill to his right, somewhere along the highway. He didn't know who lived in it, but he'd seen it. It must be ahead of him, and if he could see it, he could make it there on foot.

He finally made it off the bridge, crossing to the left side of the road to be in a better position to see the house when he came to it.

He gripped one of his ears with his bare palm. He got a moment's comfort as he walked, but as he moved his hand from ear to ear, crossing his arm in front of his face, he misstepped. His boot hit a stone, sending him teetering toward the guardrail. The steel edge caught his left knee with a stabbing, tearing sensation. He bent, rubbing the wound, a cold line drawing itself down his calf. He sat on the guardrail and leaned over his bracing arm. A dark dot spread over his jeans.

He sat and pressed it, squeezing his knee as tightly as his stiff hand would allow. The cold seemed to burn now. But sitting and resting rejuvenated him. Through the cloud of his breath, he looked across the road and up, searching for the lines and angles that defined a building, any vestiges of electric light. But the hills were only white and jagged. Tiered shadows hung where rock stood out from the snow. The hilltop was lost in clouds.

You gotta get going, pal. He stood on the pain and cussed

himself for sitting. Hobbling forward, after a few yards the stiffness seemed to give way, but the ache continued to stretch through his knee as if pulled on twine. This new slower pace stirred a mixture of anger and angst that gelled between his gut and chest. The cold air burned his throat.

He walked on, holding an image of a lighted house in his cold head. He watched the road, and he watched the hills. To his left, also, he knew that eventually there would be pastures and fences, like his own place. If he could make it, he would find his neighbors. He hated looking at the road because it always seemed to stretch, like the bridge, his steps becoming more laborious.

After looking up at the hills for the house, he was startled to discover a moose across the road, a few yards behind him. A cow, her dark coat glimmering as if in bright moonlight. She stood motionless, legs aligned and at rest, watching him. He stopped.

They stood there looking at each other silently for a moment, as if one of them had said something revelatory during an argument. Then she stepped forward, slowly into the road. Craig ached everywhere, but his head hurt particularly, to watch the moose crossing toward him. He dared not run. The moose took her time, head bobbing lightly with each step.

"I'm sorry!" The words came out flat. Craig's voice seemed to be absorbed by the snow. But the moose stopped. In the middle of the highway, she stood and blinked. The snow didn't stick to her shiny coat, the flakes seemed to go through it. Craig couldn't understand it, but still it made sense to him to have shouted the way he did.

He figured he'd be safe with one slow step. Maybe two. But it took so much effort to move. Standing was much more restful than walking. Lying down would be even better. He turned from the moose and stepped away, slowly. Again, he looked forward and up, for the house on the hill. After four or five steps, he paused to catch his breath. He turned and found the moose behind him. She had come to his side of the road and was following a few yards behind. When he stopped, she stopped.

He could no longer feel his ears, but he didn't mind. At least they didn't burn anymore. His collarbone still ached, but it was dull, and if he held his left arm against his chest like he'd been doing, the pain was manageable, like a pulled muscle. His whole frame was tired.

A glow ahead. Across the road, on a hill in the distance, there was a light. But it failed to strengthen him. There was light ahead of him and a moose behind, but his body did not want to do more than required. It didn't care about the light or the moose. It wanted rest. If it could rest a few minutes, then it would have the strength to get to the light.

So Craig sat in the snow a few feet from the side of the road. His butt did not feel the cold. But his legs felt light—an ecstasy at being released of their burden. The moose stopped and watched as Craig shifted himself into a position where he could lie down.

He propped his back gently against a rock and felt a slight complaint from his shoulder and collarbone. But it was not enough to thwart the overwhelming comfort that settled over him.

He heard his heartbeat in his head. It sounded like someone walking in hard, crusty snow, the crunch of it slow, constant, and reliable. The warmth that came next did not surprise him. He was beyond surprising. When he closed his eyes, the colors that came seemed completely natural. Wheels of green and purple and orange. Lots of red, too, large fireworks of it. There were blocks that looked like blue bales of hay. They *were* hay bales, bound together by twine that was glow-in-the-dark green. A bull elk appeared in full camo. It walked but did not walk on anything.

He would have liked something to eat. In his mind his stomach was a large, empty cave. There could be echoes in it. But he only wanted to rest. His head slipped from the rock, and he rolled slowly onto his right shoulder. His face landed on the snow, and it was like a quilt. It was the best position he'd felt in hours. His legs extended as if he were home in bed. He was home in bed, sleeping on his side. Sharlene behind him, creeping up to spoon. This. Was. Wonderful. So. Restful.

Then Sharlene spoke to him. He heard her voice, but he couldn't understand her words. Her voice caressed him. Something was humming. Something familiar was humming and Sharlene was talking. Sharlene was touching him. Sharlene was putting their blanket over him. She was tucking it around him. Sharlene was holding his head.

"Hi, sweetie," he said. "I've missed you." Craig thought he smelled coffee. He wondered why there would be coffee.

"Hello, there," she said. "*You* missed *me?* You never called, so I called. Just like I said. And you didn't answer. So here we are."

"How are the girls?"

There was a long silence. "The girls are fine. Just fine."

He opened his eyes, and the brightness of the light pained him. It was the bright light that was humming. But in front of the light was Sharlene. Her face was in the shadow, but he saw her hair. She turned and said something to someone, and in the light he thought he saw her lips, her nose, her eyebrows. In the light he saw the holly berry necklace.

"Your sister has a necklace just like yours." It seemed he had to press the words through his mouth with his tongue.

"Well, she used to have one." She held the necklace. "Mom gave one to both of us for Christmas when we were back in high school. But a day later Sharlene lost hers snowmobiling in Star Valley. Go figure. When we were kids, mom was always doing the twinner thing—you know, buying us the same clothes, same jewelry and stuff. We finally had to tell her to knock it off. Nice necklace, though. Kinda sentimental now. Here you go." Her fingers touched his chin. "Try some of this."

He smelled coffee again. He tasted its sweetness as it passed over his lips. Its warmth trickled down his throat. The light was still humming. "Thank you for coming to get me," he said, "you're just like your sister."

She held his head again. Her arm went beneath his shoulders, and she lifted him upright. "C'mon, dear. We're takin' you home."

THE RIPPLE EFFECT

by Samantha Grabler

At the seam of lake and sky,
the morning's stillness is pierced
by an oar, drenched in duality.

A single subconscious stroke
ignites the motion of thought,
displacing the water's cohesion.

Whispering, transient lines
of conjecture and opinion,
ripple outward, fragmenting
the reflection on the lake.

Confined by pattern,
the concentric circles
weave into each other,
colliding until they
cancel and collapse,
where they fade back
into stillness once more.

COIN IN THE WAVE'S RETURN

by Veronica Tucker

I tossed a coin into the ocean

not for luck

but to see what the water would do with it.

It spun once,

caught sunlight like a promise,

then vanished.

Somewhere beneath the surface,

currents argue over direction.

Even the smallest things drift for years

before they settle.

I wonder if it will ever be found

by a child ankle-deep

who thinks it's treasure,

or by a diver skimming sand

for something lost.

Maybe it will press against coral,

whispering stories in a language

no one teaches.

Or maybe it will return

to shore one day,

nudged by tide and time,

as if to say

I was never yours

but I never left.
I walk the same beach sometimes
pretending not to look.
But I feel for it
the way we all feel
for something thrown in
without a plan
a hope,
a hurt,
a half-formed question
waiting
to be answered
by waves.

A SELF-ACTUALIZED THOUGHT

by Khris Golder

Tomorrow grazes my shoulder

Having slept so little as of late

Guilty of drinking too much coffee

Ultimately I meander while

Occlusive moments

Hastily destroy these

Tacit thoughts

Delicious

Everyday failures now

Zip by

I

Leave

Alone to prepare my

Understanding of everything

Tackling each challenge

Completely free

As I now set adrift

Feelings of uncertainty

Leaving behind

Endeavors of the heart

Sometimes hinders me from

Appreciating the small wins

Going, Going
by Diana Salas-Deitch

GOING, GOING

by Shira Musicant

The doctor sits behind his desk and tells me that I am a bus terminal. He must be an expert in this because I see travel brochures and maps of city streets and timetables laid out on the large mahogany surface.

"Look," the doc says. He turns his computer toward me and shows me my outline on the screen. I see lines traveling my legs and arms, my head and torso. They are different colors, green and blue and red. I see orange and yellow. I am quite colorful, beautiful, really, all my different bus lines. I follow the green line with my eyes. It goes up my left leg and around my ribs, up my neck and circles my head then back down my neck where it converges and tangles in my torso with other lines in a messy jumble.

"You're the ending of a journey," the doc says in a tour-guide voice, pointing to my busy, tangled center. "Or the beginning of a new one. You know the saying: All roads lead to Rome." I hear admiration in his voice. "You, Sir, are host to so many passengers. They are proliferating as I speak."

He changes the image on the screen. A ticket counter, vending machines, and benches for waiting are all located in the central torso area, my tangled center. But I cannot see travelers. "Where are the passengers?" I ask. "Who are they?"

"Oh, too many to name. In fact, you are constantly adding new routes to accommodate the increase in travelers, their families, their luggage. They take over the terminal. You've become quite the host."

He turns the computer back to face him, searches around, and pulls up another scan, then turns it back to me. "See? Busy tourists." He chuckles.

Now I see the little visitors. Some pull tiny roller cases and move quickly from one colorful line to the next, changing buses, I presume. Some seem to be napping on a rib. Some are queued up at a restaurant where my spleen might have been. Some are gobbling greedily inside the restaurant.

The doctor's face turns grave. "There is a problem." He taps the computer screen. "You have no room for more buses or more bus lines. You're not able to accommodate the new travelers who keep arriving." He shows me a bus on the screen disgorging passengers who queue up at other buses, pushing each other to get a seat.

"Can you help, Doc?"

He shakes his head. "We haven't been able to stop the growing numbers of your little passengers. I've made announcements over your loudspeakers, trying to slow them down, but they continue to multiply."

"Is this serious? What's going to happen?"

"They'll probably have to build a new terminal. And yes, overcrowding is serious."

"What will happen to me?"

"Oh." The doctor shrugs, lifts his palms. "That is a question for the City Planners." He looks up at the ceiling. "I am not a philosopher, so I cannot really tell you. But they'll probably condemn you and tear you down."

The doctor clasps his hands over his generous belly and leans back in his chair. "But what will you do now? That is the real question." He picks up a travel brochure. "You won't have to stay here any longer so you might prepare for a trip."

"With the family?"

"Oh, your wife will be coming along soon enough, I imagine. The kids much later." Another one of his chuckles. "But this is a solo journey."

Now I feel a sense of urgency in the terminal as travelers rush to catch their bus and crowd on. I hear announcements, apparently important, but all inaudible. One after another.

The words blur on the front of the brochure, but I take it from him and leave his office.

***

At home I sit at our kitchen table. I tell my wife that I seem to have developed a taste for travel and that this time, she must stay at home, care for the children.

She asks where I'm going. I pull the brochure from my pocket to show her, and rest on the kitchen chair, already in demolition mode, ready for my journey. My wife and children wave goodbye. They're holding signs saying bon voyage and balloons of all different colors, green and blue and red. Orange and yellow. So many colors.

POLITE CONVERSATION

by Kunal Basu

I open my mouth to say Hello, order a coffee –
Bring me a Cinnamon latte, and top it up
With cream. I ask
For demerara sugar, and praise the sun on a November day.
My neighbour wants the Wi-Fi code, which I know by heart
Try *cafelemur* or *cafelemur21,* unless they've changed it now –
He shows me the thumb; I open my mouth to say
Have a good one.

Will you stop at Green Mamma's? – I ask the driver
Or skip the stop and cross the Hudson in one go.
The traffic is light, there's none waiting for the bus.
He waves at a friend passing by. It is still early,
for the schools and for work; Today's Sunday my friend! –
He laughs, makes me feel like a fool.

No one comes this early except you –
The lady hands me a packet at the mailbox.
She has her make-up on. A date? – I am
Tempted to ask, but keep my mouth shut. I show her a
    Lincoln'59 –
Stamps I buy for my collection. She smiles.

My grandfather had an album too. We gave it away
To the Salvation Army shop after he died.

I open my mouth to say Thank You and Never Mind, It's A
    Lovely Day, and
Yes, It Looks Like It's Going To Rain. Everyone knows what
    I'd say
Even when I keep my mouth shut.

Getting off the bus, I met this man from Kurdistan
Refugee, asylum seeker, illegal, call him what you want
He crossed the street with me
Kept walking, even though I tried to shake him off.
Scratching his beard, he told me he'd fled a war
Lived in a detention camp; lost a child
He asked me the meaning of grief

I told him about a December night, when
Mother had left me in a shelter, and I'd woken up among
Less than saintly men.

It was a long story, but I felt I must tell
The man from Kurdistan, because he'd asked. Then one thing
Led to another: we left the road for the trampled grass; shared
A cigarette – he had just the one left, and I'd quit last month.
I laughed because he didn't know what being dead-ass meant
He taught me how to say *kêfî* – their word for celebration

Listen, listen carefully – the man from Kurdistan said
And you'll hear wedding bells

We didn't say Good Night before we left

SELF

by Christopher Buckley

after the self-portrait by Ruth Leaf

Scoured by time,
by light that has almost
finished with me,
my face edged
in black & white,
woodcut or old
linoleum, unvarnished
as age, which,
with luck, with irony,
will find us all...

But this is not
what you were
expecting;
not luminance or lilies,
not a wild fantasia
of flowers.
　　The time
I've spent on my work
is time spent on my life...
This is the way

I see it, undisguised,
not a grey field
turned bright,
      briefly
with red or yellow poppies
in spring…just
the worn essential facts,
the work
made plain…
ink and grain,
all there's left
to offer, a scraping
down to bone—
after the leaf smoke
and end to autumn…

OWL AND SURGEON

by Wendy Jean MacLean

Silently present, the owl watches
as the surgeon makes precise incisions
in the stilled body.
The owl hovers on a scaffold
made of sticks and stones
and names that no one dared say.
Expert at detecting the movement
of small things, Owl watches,
ready to swoop into the hollows
to grasp its prey
with fierce confidence
in the order of life.
Owl breathes sky into the wound,
healing with ancient wisdom
that defies prognosis.
Was that a tumor or a mouse?

The Getaway
by Diana Salas-Deitch

8 8

THE GETAWAY

by Juyanne James

Two fine sisters stepped out of their Nissan Sentra like they could never be planted, anywhere. Certainly not up under some man, not being slapped around by some man, not holding on to six children ages one through eight, again, for some man. They were simply two bold, independent women, holding on tight to their pocketbooks—one slinging the purse over her plump shoulder, then clutching it, one pulling her pants up tight around her ass with one hand and holding on to her purse with the other hand. One moved just ahead of the other, with confidence, like she knew the other was following close behind her. They walked into the Dollar Store like they owned it, like they were in a hurry to make some last-minute purchases.

Exactly five minutes later, both women came rushing out of the store—one with a gun raised, pointed to heaven, the other holding on tight to newfound money, some of the bills not quite concealed within the yellow plastic bag. The heavier set one moved slower of course, her large set of breasts bounced from side to side like wings that had grown fat and lazy. The other turned just in time to see the store's security guy come chasing after them. He was a young man with a face like he'd been locked in his bedroom for years and was now out and ready to do some living. He had his gun out, too.

"Move, Mika! There the man is already. Get in the car!" The one holding the gun said all this. She had slowed by now and was setting herself up to return fire if fired upon.

Instead of continuing unabated and therefore maintaining her speed, the sister who was holding the Dollar Store bag of money tried to look back, like Lot's wife perhaps, while still running, again, with those breasts flopping, like they had a mind of their own. This caused her to lose her balance just enough to trip herself up. Then she was rolling forward on the ground, almost like she was bodysurfing or learning how to breakdance. The money bag never left the tight grip of her fingers though. It's just that now the security guy was catching up because the other sister had to stop pointing her weapon at him and, instead, reach down and help her sister get up from the ground. This was a heavy endeavor, though. The sister on the ground was still trying to recover—there was so much to do. Like sit herself upright first, then think briefly of how she could hurriedly get up from the ground, then shift her body in a sort of downward dog position before pushing herself up, still while holding tight to the yellow bag of money, then grabbing her purse, which was now lying there on the ground next to her.

The sister holding the gun was beginning to lose her patience, as any observer could see. The angst shot across her face in generous waves. Her eyes tried to do the impossible: hold on to her sister's progress while at the same time waving her gun at the security guy, who was getting too close.

"Mika, get on your ass," the impatient sister said. "Before I have to shoot somebody."

***

When the security guy heard the woman say she was going to "shoot somebody," he slowed his roll; his instinct jumped into full gear. There was a large, ill-colored trash can—like every giant receptacle that gets placed outside such establishments. The security guy could see it out of the corner of his eye. He thought of taking cover there, but noted that the trash can looked like it was made of plastic, and no matter if it was full to bursting over with trash, it would never stop a bullet traveling at bullet speed. But it might slow down the bullet's progress, the guy thought. Then his eyes caught sight of a baby oak tree—one that had obviously been planted by the chain store to provide shade and perhaps a bit of natural beauty to the otherwise barren street corner. The security guy also briefly considered the irony that the chain store had leveled the entire block and cut down the natural landscape—which included large, ancient trees that would have been perfect as cover—and had only re-added the smaller trees after the building had finally been constructed.

By now, the sister on the ground was actually pushing herself up to standing position. This time, she did not turn to look back but, rather, began a slow trot towards the car.

The other sister placed her full gaze toward the security guy and pointed her gun in his direction. This was difficult because she, too, had resumed her run, in a sideways, awkward kind of hop. She glanced at the car and, based on the look on her face, she wished they had parked it closer. But in their considered, logical minds, the chain store architects had purposefully placed the parking at the back side of the store, deciding instead on a cleaner, less cluttered look for the front of their establishment. Not to mention, the entrance to the parking was now off a main and busy street. The sisters were close, though. Another twenty yards and they could plop down in their car, race the motor, place it in gear, and then get away.

This is when both sisters heard the sirens.

***

The security guy heard the sirens as well. He questioned how the cops were en route to him so soon since response time in New Orleans was typically closer to an hour, and not the minutes since the store was robbed. The security guy welcomed the sirens, though. Now he'd have assistance in apprehending the two thieves. He felt an aroused sense of righteousness, like he had needed someone like the cops to come along and give him a pat on the back for having chased these women out of the store rather than simply letting them go. No one would blame him if he had to "shoot somebody" in the meantime. He felt justified. He might later chide himself for even questioning his motives, for feeling the need to have people give him permission to act.

The sisters, too, wondered why the cops were going to arrive so soon, and they briefly thought that perhaps this wasn't their day. Were the police officers nearby and heard the call? Either way, the sisters began to consider their options should they not get to the car and get away scot-free. They could hunker down behind the hidden side of the car, like they'd seen people do in shootouts in the movies or on TV—but that seemed a bit drastic. They could jump in the car, then give a quick call to their old men—but neither really had an old man, just a handy man they called for tune-ups, as they liked to say. They had undertaken the task of stealing from the Dollar Store on their own, reasoning that stealing the store's money was the only way to solve their immediate money troubles. They had expected that it would be an easy run-in and run-out type of situation, and that the store had plenty of money—the store had certainly taken enough of their money over the few years since it had planted itself so boldly in yet another poor neighborhood.

The sirens wailed closer.

***

The security guy decided against bravery, at least until the cops actually arrived. He was now scrunched down behind the trash can, with his eyes peeping over the top and the hand with the gun sitting and pointing, waiting for something to happen.

The sister with the bag of money was actually making progress. Almost at the car, she began to think about her classes at the local community college. The money would now cover what she owed. She could save her schedule. Not once did she consider the irony of her situation—becoming a thief and all, and, if they got caught, she'd be unavailable for classes since she'd likely be in jail.

The sister with the gun had turned and now ran at a faster pace. Seeing the security guy hunched all cowardly behind the trash can gave her courage and a newfound belief that they were going to make it. She placed the siren sounds out of her mind, even though the cops were surely only a block or so away.

Actually, the cop car, with the sirens blaring, was coming pretty fast. Too fast. Like it wasn't going to slow down in time to make the turn into the Dollar Store's parking lot, or even to slow down enough to park on the street. The car was at once upon them and then gone just as quickly. It sped by so fast that the security guy barely had a chance to stand up and raise his hands in excitement. So fast that surely the police officers inside the car never even had a chance to look out the window and see the guy jumping up and down screaming, "Stop, stop!"

And surely the police officers didn't see the two sisters, now just a few feet away from their Nissan, feeling the fear but moving even faster. The officers also did not hear the sound of their car alarm's double "beep" before unlocking the car doors. These things happened, though.

And furthermore, the sisters made quick to throw their purses in the back seat as they slid into their car seats—the heavyset one driving, and the one with the gun in the passenger seat, taking the yellow bag of money from her sister's tight grip and storing it beneath her.

***

The security guy was also surprised to hear the sound of the Nissan revving up and being placed into gear. With his full attention on the women in the car, he then revved up his courage and began to run at full pace once again, with his gun pointing, leading the way. He did not hear his manager, who had come from the store and was now shouting, "Let them go, Marvin!" He heard nothing, not even the sound of his Jordans on the pavement; his muffled breathing had closed his ears to the outside noise.

The sisters pulled up to the exit of the parking lot and waited to jump into traffic. Surely, one or both of them wondered why they hadn't planned all this at a less busy hour of the day, any time other than rush hour traffic.

The security guy was now close enough to yell, "Get out of the car! I'll shoot."

The sister holding the gun turned as much as she could

toward the window, and placed the hand holding the gun on the door's ledge. The gun was actually pointed right at the guy.

He stopped dead in his tracks, as they say. Not for fear or anything, but because everything started to make sense around him. Where at first he couldn't even hear the sound of the traffic, or the sound of the few bystanders who were near and yelling so many different things that none of it made sense, now he could hear all of it quite clearly. But the main thing he heard was the store manager saying, "No, Marvin. Let them go, Marvin!" He turned and saw the manager rushing to him, like it was life or death.

When the manager caught up to him, he bent over at his waist and placed his hands on his knees. Breathing heavy, he said, once again, "It's okay, Marvin, let them go. We've got everything on camera."

Marvin watched as the Nissan pulled out into the street and drove away. His eyes met those of the woman holding the gun. He recognized her from when she had first come into the store. She had seemed nice because when he smiled at her, she didn't turn away like some girls did when they saw him. For a second or two, he had jumped his imagination into a world where they might date, where she'd be his girlfriend. She was certainly fine enough. Her tight jeans weren't all that fashionable, but they fit her curves, showed what she was "workin' with," as they say. When she had disappeared back in the grocery area, he'd almost followed her, just to check her out, but a customer he had been watching had moved to the other side of the store. When he'd heard someone shouting that the store was being robbed, he had simply jumped into action and gone chasing after the culprits. How could he not have noticed it was her?

Perhaps because she had initially become a goddess in

his mind, and therefore, incapable of suddenly becoming a criminal, pointing a gun at him. More than anything, these were the thoughts that made him feel bad as he watched the Nissan pull away.

Little did he know, the woman in the car, the sister who had been holding the gun, was thinking about him as well. She, too, remembered the smile he had given her. He seemed so sweet she'd almost grabbed Mika by the arm and said, "No, let's not do this." But there was no turning back. Mika needed the money. She had worked so hard to get accepted into college, only to hear the woman at the payment window say she was short by hundreds of dollars. They had pooled all the money they had, even sold whatever they could, but they didn't have the money. The robbery had been her idea, not Mika's. Mika was the smarter sister, the more trustworthy one; that's why she was going to make something of herself. She was going to be somebody. So, as the car moved down the street, all the while trying to fit in with traffic and not draw attention, the sister who had been holding the gun thought about Mika, and then she thought about the security guy.

The two fine sisters didn't stop at their house, but instead drove straight to the college and applied the money to her account. They had about fifty dollars left over.

"Put it toward books," her sister said.

And that's what Mika did.

WALK LIKE YOU

for Nathan

by Peter Schwartz

nobody can tell anybody else how

to walk but please

walk however you decide all the way

walk as if from a ditch

walk with that extra light from your parents' steady in
    your eyes

walk with so little limp in your step others can find
    strength on your road

walk as if there is no chance of an avalanche and even if
    there is so what

walk like you're always being mutated into something
    better

walk like your sweat has value

walk like the rain has answers too

walk like a porcupine who has mastered adrenaline

walk like the opposite of camouflage and shine
    correspondingly

walk like there is no great silencer

walk away from the flies towards better invitations

walk like every step was worth it from the beginning

and never stop

MOTHER

by Christine Jackson

Lately you are there,
or rather, here
seeping through old sediment,
a slow but steady trickle of ancestral plasma.

You begin to pool, to take up space,
to make your putative self known.
You brown spot me and turn my hair white.
You lock me in a chair—hip, ham, and hock.
I close my eyes and invite the seepage.

The waters rise slowly.
Soaking my tired bones
Filling secret chambers
Until I brim and pour
Through the floorboards
To the scrubby earth below.

I am older now, not entirely senescent,
But old enough to see the warp and weft of a life.
Born of you and your mother, and her mother and hers,
To recognize the intercellular matrix of what was, what is,
    and what will be.

We are theme and pattern
Unfinished story
Recurrent and revelatory

Mother-past and daughters-future
You bracket the timeless passing of this life.
My slow drowning in an epigenetic pool of eternal return.

Mysterious Way
by Diana Salas-Deitch

DREAMCHILD

by Eugene Datta

She'll have your hair, he said, and your skin, she said, and your arching eyebrows. Your eyes, said he, and your lovely lips. And she's got to have that vein on her forehead, she said, and he agreed because that's the one thing they had in common. But the nose—the nose remained undecided: she said his, he said hers, and they left it at that. She'd have their love for books, they decided, and she'd learn to breathe water like a mermaid and music like her mother. A couple of names were tossed around. And there she was, their dreamchild. Whose nose she had didn't seem to matter.

Awkward Paws
by Diana Salas-Deitch

AWKWARD PAWS

by Nathan Loceff

It had not been my intention to steal the cat. I didn't want, nor did I have the space for, a cat. I live in a small studio apartment on the fifth floor, so there isn't really anywhere for a cat to play, or to do whatever it is cats do all day. Plus, it was my close friends' new cat. Still a kitten, really. Not that it makes a great deal of difference how old the cat is. I also had no good way of transporting the cat from their apartment in Rouen back to mine in Paris.

As my friends had instructed me, I dropped the keys into the mailbox as I left. I wasn't sure what I would say when one of them called me to tell me the cat was gone. Was I to pretend it had escaped as I left, or pretend it was there in the apartment when I left, or was I to admit right away that I had catnapped the thing?

Now is as good a time as any to say that the cat only has three legs. The mother ate the leg by mistake during kittenbirth.

Apparently, at least my friends would have me believe, this is quite common. Why anyone would want a three-legged cat is beyond me, or I guess it isn't because I have one now. But I am not sure I want it. I don't know what came over me when I was leaving. I said goodbye to it, and it just sat there looking at me. I had almost closed the door behind me, but then I pushed it open again, and the little kitten had not moved. It was just sitting there staring right at me and in that moment I felt pity for it. I felt I couldn't leave it there in the apartment by itself. I must have lost my mind.

As the train sped from Rouen to Paris, I sat there watching the sunset over barren trees and empty fields with my cat contraband in my backpack on the seat next to me. Here and there stood horses, cows, sheep in the fields. At that moment though, they all looked like oversized and misshapen cats to me.

When the people sitting near me on the train began looking around to find the source of all the meowing, I thought I'd better offer up an explanation before anyone realized I had a three legged kitten hidden away in my backpack. So, I announced quite nonchalantly that it was just my ringtone. When some faceless person told me to turn my phone to silent, I said that unfortunately, it was broken and I could do no such thing. When a few minutes later someone else, or perhaps the same person, suggested that I just turn the damn thing off I decided to ride the rest of the journey in the space between the two cars where people are allowed to make phone calls.

As the train rocked back and forth and I stood there with the cat in my backpack it was becoming clearer and clearer that I should not have stolen my friends' new cat. If there had been some reason, any reason at all, for taking the cat, it would have been different. I could have explained these hardships away as necessary inconveniences for the good of the greater plan, but I had no plan at all. Plus, as soon as I arrived in Paris I had a date, and no time to bring the cat home first. It was a first date.

When we eventually arrived, I got off the train like everyone else, and suddenly the ridiculousness of my situation hit me. I had a three-legged cat in my backpack. It made me think, what kind of bizarre things do the people around me have in their backpacks, suitcases, purses? As I was walking through the seething mass of bodies in St. Lazare, my phone rang. It was the rightful owner of the cat on the other end. I didn't know what to do and then my indecision made the choice for me. One missed call from rightful cat owner. I had a date to get to; other things, such as uncomfortable phone conversations didn't concern me. I went down to the metro and took line 14 to our appointed meeting place. The Bibliothèque François Mitterrand station. We were planning to meet at one of my favorite cafes in the 13th, in a neighborhood where I used to live.

The metro was loud and crowded; no one could hear the pleading meows of my kitten this time. Or if they could, the city effect was in full swing. On a train taking you from one city to another you know you have to sit there with the people around you for the whole journey and you know approximately how long the journey will take. And so you become mildly interested in your allotted train time. Maybe you even plan on doing work, or reading. On the metro however, people come and go every minute, you don't have a seat, you are already so uncomfortable you think to yourself I'll just get to where I'm going and then I'll be a person again. Metro time doesn't really exist; it is a troglodytic temporal void.

When I got out at Bibliothèque François Mitterrand I opened the backpack to check on my burden. He looked uncomfortable. Or was I projecting? He simply stared up at me with his darling little eyes, and I realized that I really was in love. I looked at my watch. It was 7:06. Where was my date? I looked around and then realized we had planned to meet in the cafe, so in fact it was I who was late. I rushed down the street toward the cafe. It is situated on a corner that butts up against a wall and there are no other restaurants or bars that can be seen from the street, so approaching it always gives me the feeling that I am seeking out the only shelter in a vast wilderness of concrete. That night in the dark and cold, as soon as it came into view, with its warm light dripping out into the street and with the little group of smokers standing around the doorway, I felt that I was pulling into a foggy harbor at the moment when dusk turns to night after being out in the damp sea air for far too long. I was wet and smelled of fish and my hands were caked with salt. All of that was inconsequential though, because the most important thing was that I was tired, dead tired. The dock promised repose and that promise was a beautiful thing in and of itself. I was ready to dock my boat and go into a little restaurant for a hot bowl of chowder. Why I felt like a fisherman I can't say. I've never even been on a boat, nor have I ever lived near the sea; where had these images come from? Probably television. Or maybe I was starting to commune with the cat in my bag. Cats after all are basically fishermen.

As I got close to the cafe I saw her there, already at a table near the window. I rushed in. We kissed hello on the cheek as people do in this country and as my cheek came close to hers I

hoped it was a bit of foreshadowing for the rest of the night's adventure.

We ordered beer and started to talk.

Of course she heard the cat's meows, and metaphorically the cat was out of the bag even if physically it was still in the bag.

When I showed her how cute it was she asked:

"What's its name?"

"It doesn't have one yet, but I was thinking of calling it Awkward Paws because it only has three legs and when it walks around it's a bit awkward.

She laughed.

"Yeah, I don't usually like puns, but this one is just too perfect."

"Why don't you have one of those cat-carrying bags for it?

"Well, it wasn't my plan to get a cat. I just found this particular cat adorable, and I couldn't say no."

She smiled.

The cat continued to howl in distress.

"It doesn't seem to like being cooped up in there," she said

"Well, I don't blame it. I simply didn't have time to go back home on my way from Rouen. I didn't want to be late meeting you."

"Not much of a planner, huh?"

"Well..."

"I'm just kidding," she said with a smile. Then she took a sip of beer and continued, "I'm not being forward and I don't want you to read into this, but I live quite close to here and I think after we finish this drink we should go to my place for a second drink; that way we can let the cat run around. I don't want to make the little guy suffer," she paused and smiled, "and I also don't want to prematurely end our date."

As we walked down the street, the two of us and the cat, I

touched her hand and not only did she let me take it in mine, but she turned toward me and we kissed very briefly and then kept walking hand in hand. As we passed the laundromat where I used to dry my clothes in winter, I felt like we were a happy family, man, woman and cat.

"Wow, this is such a nice place," I said as we stepped into her apartment.

And it was true. The apartment was huge. It had two living rooms, a kitchen and even a balcony. It was amazing. I had never seen such a nice apartment in Paris. It was the kind of place that would be nice even if it wasn't in Paris.

We let the cat out. It immediately started to run around the room. Then it dashed into one of the other rooms.

"Do you want some tea?" she asked, "I'm a little cold."

"Sure."

She went into the kitchen and I followed the cat into the other room. It was sitting on a couch and I sat next to it and began caressing it, taking in the room around me. She had a huge bookshelf that took up an entire wall. I went over to have a look at the titles. I was standing there when the lights went out.

"What happened?" she yelled.

"What?"

"The lights."

"I don't know."

"Can you come here?"

"Does this happen often?" I shouted as I tried to make my way to the kitchen.

"No, actually it's never happened before."

When I made it into the kitchen I saw her in the semi-darkness from the streetlamps outside. We both laughed.

108

"Some first date!" I exclaimed, "if things go well, we'll have a funny story to tell our kids."

I don't know why I said this, and I couldn't tell in the darkness if she found it charming or deranged.

"So, where's the fuse box?"

"I don't know, I haven't lived here that long and like I said, this hasn't happened before."

I decided to just take the moment in hand, so I held her to me and kissed her. We were standing there kissing and then we heard the cat meow. We looked down and it was right at our feet.

"Ok, we better get the lights back on," she said.

She used the flashlight on her phone, we found the fuse box, flipped the fuse back, but it just went back down again immediately.

"What were you doing when the lights went out?" I asked.

"Cutting apples."

"Well, that certainly wouldn't blow a fuse. What else were you doing?"

"Umm, oh, boiling water for the tea."

"Where's the kettle?"

She pointed her phone, and I saw water all over the table where the kettle was sitting. "Shine it under there," I said, and we both got down on our hands and knees. There was water all over the floor.

"I see what happened. There was too much water in the kettle and it spilled onto the power strip, and that must have blown the fuse." I reached over and unplugged the power strip.

"Ok, try and hit the fuse again," I said.

She got up and walked back to the fuse box, flipped the switch, and the lights came back on.

"Voila!" she said with enthusiasm.

I unplugged the kettle from the power-strip and plugged it directly into the wall and...

***

Well, this is quite awkward; our narrator just got electrocuted and died. If we want to continue to follow the sad state of affairs that our three-legged friend finds itself in, we must take a step back from the point of view we have thus far been inhabiting. And let's hurry, the story is almost over. The woman stood there in shock staring at the body lying lifeless on her floor. She felt something brushing against her left leg. Looking down she saw that the kitten had hobbled up to her and was rubbing against her affectionately. She reached down, picked it up and held it to her chest. She looked into its tiny eyes. It really was irresistible. For a split second, it held her entire attention, and it was as if there was no dead man lying a few feet away from her. It was just her and the kitten locked in a comforting stare. Then the phone in the man's pocket buzzed and the woman gave a short high-pitched scream. This startled the cat, who jumped out of her arms and landed on the man's back before running off into another room.

The man's phone buzzed again. She could see which pocket it was in as the screen lit up. Not knowing what else to do she took a breath, reached down and put her hand into the pocket. She felt the smooth touch of the screen and it vibrated again. She fished it out, stood up and put it to her ear. Immediately, a voice responded, "Finally, why haven't you been picking up? I've been calling all day!"

She had answered the phone for the same reason she had picked up the kitten. She didn't want to be alone. She wanted, no, needed help with the situation she was in, a situation that seemed completely insane. But for some reason the voice on the other end of the line didn't seem like the right voice, there was something about it that let her know immediately it was not going to provide the help she needed. So, when after a pause the voice said: "Hello? HELLO?" she decided not to respond.

By this time the kitten had returned and was again rubbing her leg. It meowed. There was silence on the other end of the line.

The kitten meowed again.

Then the voice on the other end rang out louder than before. "Is that my cat!? What the hell is…"

Before she could hear the end of the sentence, she hung up. She turned off the phone, put it in her pocket, and then reached down and picked up the kitten. She kissed it on the nose. There really was something special about it, and as she held it in her arms, she made two decisions: one, that whatever happened, she was going to keep it, and two, that its name would be Awkward Paws.

WHEN I WAS THE MOON

by Michael Spivack

When I was the moon,
I peered at the Earth,
(Majestic in her balanced incandescent glory),
Encumbered by the syrup of ideal love,
And with the cold wind of space creating a tragic and
     permanent buffer.

I grew bitter, little by little.
Grayer and grayer.
More and more envious of her colors and swirls.
And then suddenly like the changing of seasons,
I was back in her throes.
Butterflies in my core,
Filled with parabolic hope,
Perfumed with fantasy,

And each year this cycle continued
Only gradually, over eons, getting more bearable
I slowly began to accept that I was destined
to love from afar
and shine down famously from her skies
onto her beautiful oceans

and forests
and mountains
and cities
and people

In truth, I only needed that tiny fluid spot in her skies to
     leave an eternal impression of importance.

As the cycle continued,
I began to realize,
I, like you, like she, would be nothing at all without the sun

Looking Up
by Diana Salas-Deitch

LOOKING UP

by B.J. Burton

He was a builder, and when he built his own house, he installed heating coils in the ceiling because it was 1964, and he believed electricity was the heat of the future, but the problem was, it caused the plaster covering the coils to crack, collapse, and fall, so if you were standing underneath, like his children were, it was a frightening prospect at any given time, with no warning, for the ceiling to come crashing down, which, in turn caused the little ones to be in a perpetual state of high alert from looking up at all hours of the day and night, which, in turn, ended up causing sleeping difficulties, eating disorders, and anxious tendencies because what they had most feared happened over and over again; for instance, a falling chunk landed in one of the bedrooms, scaring the cat so much that she ran away, disappearing forever, and displacing the red wagtails, which found themselves in a less than liquid environment, and because the children were conditioned for so many years, even outside, their little necks were craned up toward the clouds, and even years after the house was bulldozed to dust, the children, now adults, gazed upward during the most casual of conversations, still worried about the sky.

VISITING THE HOUSE WHERE WE USED TO LIVE

by Eddi Salado

Crocus still grow
along the walkway
and that tree with the angry face
is stalwart by the fence.

Everything looks the same
from the outside—
as if, were I to open
the door, our lives would be
exactly the same

Peter Rabbit sits
on the dresser by the crib
in the baby's room.

Yellow curtains still
at the kitchen window
where the ghosts of dinners
linger like smoke.

And the names
we whispered

to each other when we
weren't shouting
cling to the floral wallpaper.

I want to pick up the phone
and call our old number,
imagine you might
answer and ask
when will you be home?

THE THIRD DIMENSION

by Samantha Grabler

I'm Triaxial,
In geometry,
This X, Y, and Z…
Caged by coordinates–
So planar, unfree

And time's forward flow,
Just won't let me go,
It's sometimes too fast…
Then, relatively too slow

There's a down direction,
That pulls with oppression,
Gravity's fixed force–
A constant compression

When force is innate,
I'm stuck at its rate,
Sunken and buried,
By pressurized weight

And, in this void,
Nothing's destroyed,

Change is the constant,
From which all is deployed

While my perception,
Is a small projection,
Of fundamentals,
Below our detection

I myself am just an extension
Of laws beyond comprehension…
I'm suffocating, blind
Stuck here, in this Third Dimension

A COAT OF MY POCKETS

by Tom Tulloh

Wrapped in a coat of my pockets,
filled up with envelopes,
you open them one by one.

Wrapped in a coat of my pockets
Inwardly helium presses the seams.
A match is struck

wrapped in a coat of my pockets
there are webs that are shapeless
but spin on beams.

Wrapped in a coat of my pockets
lie some seeds in dust and amber.
A shovel unworking scrapes.

Wrapped in a coat of my pockets
pour out a drain, a well, a wickless lamp:
let's catalogue the unspecific.

A last unravelling point—
till squints the eye drifted.
Wrapped in a coat of my pockets,
you open them one by one.

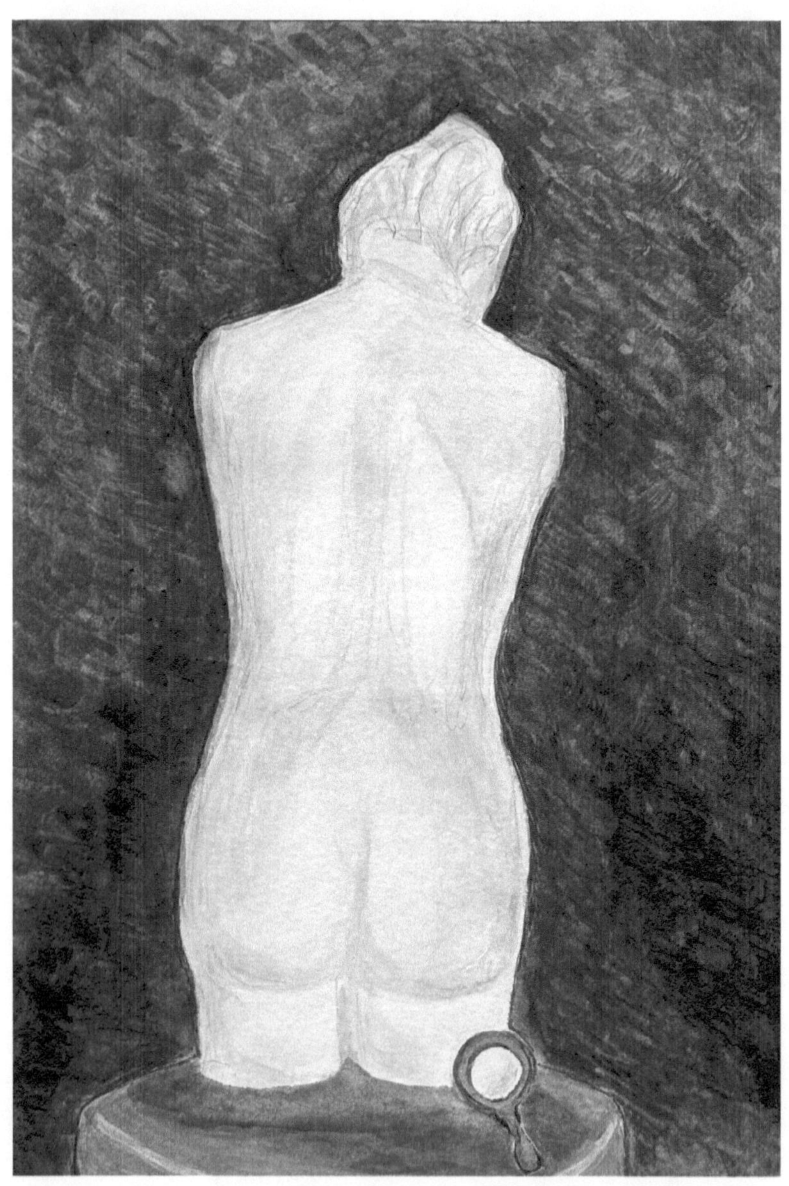

Love is a Limbless Statue
by Diana Salas-Deitch

LOVE IS A
LIMBLESS STATUE

by B. Geren Sanford

"You think it's a fake?" I roll myself closer, taking the proffered ring. Turning my attention from the exquisite art around me, I examine it, tipping my head despite my oversized bifocals. I concentrate on the crown, a carved oval amethyst incised with the head of Diogenes—our ever-cynical seeker of honesty—etched as an intaglio made to imprint the meticulous design into wax for a seal. "It's beautiful, Gavin. You suspect a forgery?"

"Oh, I know it's fake, Theo," Gavin smirks in his secretive way as he steps away from me. "Because I commissioned it," he calls back over his shoulder. Though relying on his cane, Gavin Caldwell limps his lanky frame with hustle. He locks the front door of his gallery, Contemplating Clio, flipping the window sign to close early.

"Well, if you had it made, and admit it's a fake, then it's not fraud." I lean closer to it, flicking away my long, silver mane of thick curls. "Ironic? Yes, given the subject and his moral skepticism, searching for an honest soul. But there's no crime in irony, yet."

I turn the piece over in my hand. "It's fine work." In a moment I'm roaming my memory palace, that place in my mind where I house my knowledge of art. I visualize my palace as an endless, perfect Parthenon, pristine and undamaged. I can move through here faster than in my wheelchair in the real world. Beyond the simple, fluted grooves of an exterior Doric column, I find myself in a courtyard of an ancient Roman home, circa first century BCE. I spy a similar intaglio ring on the hand of the artist I seek, and his name comes to mind in an instant. "In the style of Gnaios, right?"

Gavin nods. "It is. So, what's wrong with it?" Ever the gallerist, he adjusts his impeccable tie.

"What do you mean? It's perfect," I lie.

"Tsk-tsk, my friend," admonishing me as if I were an undergrad and not an old fart like him. "Theo, I know you too well," he smirks. "You're practically bursting to tell me."

"Fine!" I return his grin as I spin my wheelchair to offer back the ring. "The hair's right, a sense of softness difficult to capture in stone. But the skin tone is off. Too much subcutaneous muscle for Gnaios. He preferred his subject's skin like I do — nice and taut." I clap my hands together. "So, who'd you coax to craft it?"

"You know Mikahlo?"

"The young phenom of mixed media? Yeah, I've heard of him." At Gavin's raised eyebrows, I feign indignation. "What? Specializing in Classical art and antiquities doesn't make me an artifact. I've been in plenty of modern galleries other than yours."

"Contemplating Clio is eclectic, not modern."

"Ooh, touchy," I wink. "Anyway, I saw Mikahlo's clay amphoras plastered in peacock feathers. Loved it! This guy a friend of yours?"

"Working on it. We have a certain mutual interest. I convinced him to include a piece in my new art exhibit, Reflections on Love." He points to the far corner, where a Greek youth stands, kouros-style, slathered in Day-Glo acrylics. "That's why I called on you."

"You think Mikahlo didn't actually create it?"

"Not that piece. No, you're here to judge the potential *pièce de résistance* of the exhibit." He glances at his watch. "Which should be arriving any minute now."

As if on cue, the back doorbell rings. I can't deny my pulse quickens at the prospect.

"So, this delivery is what you want me to appraise? Okay, then, what can you tell me about it?"

Gavin stands up but his lips stay sealed.

"What's all the mystery, you art-tease?" We traverse the gallery toward the storeroom, each in our own way.

"All I can tell you is that the dealer, Iris Lovelace, was sworn to secrecy by the seller. I had to sign an NDA just to see the thing. But I assure you, it's worth it."

"You know I don't do NDAs!" I protest, stopping at the entrance to the back storeroom. Gavin shuffles up the two big steps that prevent me from following.

"Don't worry, old friend. I know." He turns back. "In exchange for no red tape, Iris has agreed to obtain your 'objective endorsement.' Her words. However, it is on the condition that you make your appraisal today." The bell rings again. "That was the only way I could wrangle this. Wait here." He walks away.

"Wait here? What?!?" He leaves me there unassisted as they

unload the truck beyond my sightlines. "Fuck NDAs! Instead, I should cry ADA and sue your ass back to Unwokelahoma!" I call out, even if I never would. I hate waiting, but Gavin is a dear friend who has never steered me wrong.

Truth be told, I've always admired the man and his story. So strange to think someone as groomed and cultured as Gavin was born in the Sooner State. Of course, he escaped that rural panhandle to join the Army as soon as he could. He'd almost finished a tour in Iraq for Desert Storm before shrapnel tore up his leg.

Gavin found his savior in art, much as I did. We met in New York City during the mid-nineties SoHo art scene, before it went all upscale retail. This was when the Guggenheim still had a branch there. Back then, he worked there and had been assigned to roll a certain headstrong invalid through the galleries. We soon discovered a mutual love of both art and the absurd. Gavin and I have been friends and colleagues ever since.

Gavin enters first, followed by a mover who installs a short ramp for the steps, then another who rolls a dolly down it. The cart carries a small humanoid figure swaddled in packing blankets, strapped in like a tiny Hannibal Lecter. But even beneath the covering, there's something odd about the shape, as if it had overly broad legs or a narrow pedestal.

"Well, color me intrigued," I murmur to Gavin. "Whatever the fuck color that is."

As Gavin assists the movers in placing and slowly unwrapping the miniature mummy, a raven-haired windstorm swoops into the gallery. "Be careful," she addresses the movers. "That piece is worth more than your past six generations ever made."

126

I clear my throat with drama. "I'll be the judge of that."

Iris Lovelace spins on her stiletto heels to regard me. I can't say what's most striking about her. Maybe it's her Gnaios-taut face. Or maybe it's those intense green eyes, where sapphires grow pale and emeralds blanch in comparison. Or perhaps it's that mischievous smile, as sharp as her heels, polished like Vulcan steel. Though she barely breaches 5-feet, her presence fills the room as if she owns it.

"Ah, the notorious Theo Armitage, art appraiser extraordinaire!" She hides it well, but I note her gaze lingering both lower and longer than she intends.

"Ms. Lovelace, I presume?" I wheel up to her and kiss her hand like the gentleman I'm not. Glancing down, I add, "What? Didn't Gavin tell you?"

"Well, yes. But he didn't mention…" She regards my nonexistent legs. "…such a thorough amputation." She lifts her head, locking onto my gaze. "To not even leave you any stumps?"

"You're expecting it was some accident, defending God and Country like Gavin, or some tragic childhood illness." I shrug. "Sorry to disappoint, but my pregnant mom didn't smoke; my dad wasn't absent or hit her. It just… happened. I was born this way, like a car rolled off the assembly line without any wheels." I wink and gesture to my lower half. "But I still got the leg that counts."

I expect her to blush like most, but to her credit, she doesn't. Instead, she turns with a flourish to the statue, as the last layer of wrapping is removed.

"I present to you the Aphrodite Immaculatus."

Before me stands a meter-tall marble sculpture supported by an equally tall cylindrical base. If the statue was ever complete, only its milky-white head, torso, and upper thighs remain. Its limbs are absent. The form is that of Aphrodite in the style of Praxiteles and his famous nude of Knidos. It is an evocative piece, even in its flawed state.

I'm instantly struck by the luminous marble, which could only be fine-grained Parian marble, the same as Praxiteles would've used for his lost masterpiece. I find my mind slipping into my personal Parthenon, searching my expertise in ancient Greek styles and techniques. It's constructed as a series of spaces hidden among the ornate Ionic columns that support its vast interior. I round a pillar and locate my guide, in the likeness of the elder Roman statesman, Cicero. While historical accounts picture him as "eloquence itself," I always imagine him having a bit of a sailor mouth.

Cicero's horrified eyes pin me with their directness. "What the fuck are you doing here when there are people staring at you?" And with a wave of his hand, I'm expelled.

I realize the room is quiet, with all eyes riveted on me, awaiting my first reaction. I can't help myself. What starts as a chuckle, like stones dancing on the skin of a lake, grows into fits of giggles until I explode in a full-blown braying of mirth and amusement. The movers quickly slip away, leaving Iris and Gavin to gawk.

"Immaculatus? Latin for… unblemished?" I struggle for breath between the fading snorts and snickers. "First, Gavin, it's your ring with the face of Honesty's Rottweiler. And now this: Love's limbless statue." I narrow my eyes at them. "Is this some sort of prank?"

Iris is not fazed or amused. "On the contrary. This is a rare, small-scale reproduction from the Hellenistic era, circa third to second century BCE—"

"Stop!" I hold my hand out like a traffic cop. "You're serious." I look at Gavin who slowly nods. "Okay, what's its provenance?

Iris pulls a folder from her attaché case, handing it to me. "It was recovered among a large horde of artifacts in 1859 by Sir Charles Newton, the British archaeologist." She grows more animated. "On behalf of the British Museum, he was visiting southwestern Anatolia, part of the Ottoman Empire at the time, once ancient Caria, now modern-day Turkey."

As I thumb through the folder, I picture the old port of Knidos along the coast of that region, a gorgeous view of the Mediterranean from the hills above, where the circular Temple of Aphrodite once hosted Praxiteles' famous offering to the temple, long lost to the world.

Iris continues. "This Aphrodite was sent to London, one crate among hundreds, all filled with marble statues, pottery fragments, and other verified relics."

I hold up a page. "It was catalogued as 'of questionable origin' at the time."

Gavin dabs his forehead with the handkerchief. "So, they thought it a fake?"

"No," she replies. "They were merely confused, as I presume Theo here is, by the use of Parian marble on such a reproduction. That's what makes this work so remarkable. It's thought that all the later Hellenistic and Roman copies used the golden-hued, coarse-grained Pentelic marble." She gestures to the Immaculatus. "But apparently not."

I roll backward in shock. "Are you claiming this to be an original Praxiteles? Some scale model maquette by the great master himself?"

"Isn't that what you're here to tell me?" There's that

mischievous smirk again. She's too friendly by far.

I clear my throat. Tapping a page in her folder. "You say it was deaccessioned by the British Museum, though there's no clear evidence of when or why."

"That is correct. But as you see, it appeared in the private collection of some Turkish merchant in the 1950s, and eventually found its way into the hands of the current owner, my client, about 10 years ago." She moves closer to Gavin. "As Gavin and I discussed, my client is looking for a buyer. We think this gallery, and the *Reflections on Love* exhibition in particular, is the perfect place to show it off."

I glance through the sheets. It looks convincing enough, but provenance and paperwork are all too easily faked nowadays. The truth is always found in the piece itself. Aphrodite wants to tell us her story. We just need to open our senses to learn it.

I turn my gaze back to the nude woman preparing for her bath. She makes no attempt to hide her nakedness from me. "Alright, you can leave the paperwork with me." I roll over to my briefcase. "I need two hours with her." Unsnapping the clasp, my case glides open to reveal its velvet-cradled contents. "Alone."

"Excuse me?" Iris shakes her head. "No. I'd rather stay."

I pull out my magnifying glass and black light. "Ah, but you want my authentication, and I need to work without distraction."

"What do you intend to do? You'd better not deface or defile it."

"Oh, that would be too kind." I extract my laptop and inventory my tools of the trade. "No, I'm going to Sherlock the shit out of it."

"Unacceptable! Gavin…?"

"I told you, Iris. He needs time alone to complete his work." Gavin raises a finger. "I take full responsibility. This is Theo's method, and he's one of the best." He points to the cameras around the galley. "All proceedings, from examination to appraisal determination, are being recorded, both audio and video."

He gently leads her to the door. "Besides, I know a lovely coffee shop where we can discuss the finer points of Banksy as an artistic provocateur."

Though reluctant, she's coaxed to the door. Gavin holds it open for her, then follows. But just before it closes, he glances back, holding the fake Diogenes intaglio ring aloft to me. Without a word, I understand. Then he's gone, the door locked behind him.

I smile at Aphrodite. "Okay, girl, tell me all your secrets."

***

I'm in three places at once. First and foremost, I'm in the gallery studying the superb details of the sculpture before me—the cut, texture, and form imparted upon the stone. I'm also online, digging for information that corroborates or refutes the story Iris has woven. And most importantly, I search my memory palace for where this sculpture belongs. First, I must determine several things—when and where was it carved, using what technique, why it was sculpted, and ultimately by whom, if possible.

Cicero emerges from behind a column, straightening out his white toga, bordered with a broad purple stripe to mark his status.

"Parian marble is a remarkable material," I say to Cicero as we move among the pillars of my Parthenon. "A near-translucent plasticity." In the real world, I stroke Aphrodite's smooth surface with the touch of a reverent lover.

We turn the next column and find ourselves in the Temple of Aphrodite in Knidos, the waves of the Mediterranean crashing far below. In the center stands my mind's idealized vision of the original Aphrodite masterpiece, the Knidia. It's stunning beyond description.

"Of the Knidia, they said, 'though she was of stone, it was stone set afire.' That's how they described it." Cicero turns from the ideal to face me. "How does this Aphrodite Immaculatus compare?" The two statues are now side by side and I lean in for an assessment.

"It pales. The stone is right, and the sculpting is magnificent. But I suspect it's the work of an acolyte, not the master." I can almost feel the hesitation in some of the chiseling. "And Parian marble has always been available, even if it fell out of fashion." I do a quick online search. "You can even source some today with deep pockets or a well-connected benefactor."

"So, this isn't the time period where this reproduction belongs." Cicero strides out.

"Wait up!" I race after him. As the pillars fly by, I whisper a prayer to Athena to give me wisdom and insight. When I finally catch up to Cicero, we're in the great Roman Colosseum.

In a moment, dozens of ancient Greek and Roman replicas litter the sandy floor of the amphitheater. From the Venus de Milo to the Medici Venus and all the variations between, all inspired to some degree by the Aphrodite of Knidos, the first to show the goddess nude. I place the Immaculatus among them.

***

Cicero sweeps his hand along the tops of the statues. "What do you think of the pose and expression?"

Most of the reproductions share the same gesture, with her

right hand attempting to cover her modesty. The later replicas built on this, using variations of the pudica gesture, with both hands hiding her womanhood. The resulting stance is a striking contrapposto pose, an uneven distribution of weight, with her projecting hip lending an almost languid curve to the body.

I examine the Immaculatus, moving back to take in its entirety. "There! The angle of the missing arms." I find myself pointing with both mind and body. "I'd bet my last leg that only this right arm barely tried to cover her genitalia, just as Praxiteles' Knidia was said to do."

"Good observation," he smiles. "What does that tell you?"

"Unfortunately, not much. You can't use what isn't there." I glance down at my missing limbs.

Cicero frowns. "And?"

"Well, there's still the head, turned in profile to the right, a pose as ancient as the cult of Aphrodite itself. And the face!" I peer at her countenance. "A masterful mix of contempt and mischievous sneer. This Aphrodite, she shows no shame at being discovered emerging from her bath, not like these later copies."

"Would you say this work is originating to what came after it or reacting to what came before?"

"I honestly don't know." I run my hands through my hair, staring at the ground.

I look again at Aphrodite, and this time she whispers something. *See me.* And for the first time, I really do.

"Here is pain born of desperation, a struggle to be seen. that is what I was missing!" I lower to the ground and gaze up at her hidden flower. "There must be a sign…"

And with that, I know where to enshrine this Aphrodite Immaculatus in my memory palace.

***

I'm so deep in the flow that I don't even hear them return until Gavin announces, "So Theo, what do you think of this *rara avis?*"

"It's a rare bird indeed, Gavin." I look up from my study of the texture where one of the arms has broken off. "This is truly a stunning piece. A beguiling brew of beauty and mystery."

Iris approaches, placing a hand on the goddess. "I knew it would fascinate you, Theo." Up close I catch the complex, earthy scent of her perfume. "I particularly love the enigma of its inscrutable face. That blend of knowing smile and smirk. Like an ancient herald of the Mona Lisa."

"Apples and oranges," I snap. I don't care for her hyperbole and superlatives. I roll back to the table where the dossier lay. "I noticed there's no report of a microscopy analysis performed."

"You know that wouldn't help." She dismisses the idea with a flick of her hand. "The stone could be ancient, while the carving itself more recent."

"Indeed. Though some techniques can provide insight on the degree of alteration and weathering, as well as an analysis of tool marks."

Gavin frowns. "Will you need such an analysis to determine its authenticity?" I can tell he's nervous when the houndstooth handkerchief comes out to dab his forehead.

"No. I'm confident in my examination. For example, I'm reasonably certain that the missing limbs are due to a fall or similar impact and they were not chiseled off or mechanically removed.

"Which means what? That it is authentic?" He looks uncharacteristically anxious, fumbling with his phone.

"I'm afraid it's not so simple as that."

1 3 4

"So, what is your verdict then, Theo?" Iris smiles, reeling her catch in. "Do you agree that it's genuine? A rare ancient statue of unparalleled craft?"

I glance at my friend. I know he'll be disappointed, but he needs to hear it from me. "I'm afraid I cannot agree to its authenticity."

"Why not?" Iris's voice grows cold, her eyes boring new holes in my head.

"I think you know why. But if you need it spelled out for you…"

Her eyes flick to the security camera, and the most deviously charming smile falls over her face. "The real question is: Are you sure, Theo?" She stepped closer. "Are you absolutely sure of your choice? I mean, you can ill afford another Antique Roadshow fiasco. I bet missing that masterpiece still keeps you up at night. Perhaps, you've grown gun-shy in your old age."

In my mind I see Cicero walking among us, shaking his head. "Oh, she's good. She knew right where to cut you. How to make you doubt yourself. What if it's authentic? We both know you want it to be." Cicero saunters up to the statue. "But Aphrodite speaks for herself. Tell her story."

Before I can reply, the front doorbell rings, followed by a pounding at the door. Gavin hobbles to peek through the shade. "It's Mikahlo!"

Iris turns red. *Ah, so that is the color of intrigue.*

The young artist bursts in, the epitome of agitation, his dark skin glistening with perspiration, as if he ran all the way here. One glance at the statue and his body stiffens, but not in surprise. His mouth sets tight in some kind of ominous confirmation.

"Mikahlo! Are you all right?" Gavin places a hand on his

shoulder. "What's wrong?

"Her." He points at Iris. "Gavin, when I saw you with her at the coffee shop, I feared the worst—that she was going to scam you like so many others. I've been wrestling with my conscience ever since, but decided to come forward, even if it ruins me."

"You know this statue, don't you?" I ask, but I already know. "This isn't the first time you've seen it."

The artist regards me with a nod, then fixes Iris with an accusatory gaze. "I know her and I know this statue because she commissioned me to carve it four years ago. I was a talented nobody, which was exactly what she needed for her little scam—selling it to some unsuspecting buyer as a genuine ancient Greek statue." He strides closer to me. "But the whole song and dance you gave … this statue is a replica I made at her request. And now she's trying to pull the same shit all over again!"

Fury radiates from Iris like flames. I can't help but fan them. "Is any of this true?"

"Lies!" she stammers. "It's all lies." She gets that same cunning smirk again. "And who'd believe an artist with his background? Hardly credible."

Mikahlo stammers some unintelligible reply, looking to Gavin with uncertainty.

The gallerist limps forward. "If this is true, Mikahlo, you must have some way to prove it?"

"He does." I smile. Everyone stares at me, but I'm used to it. "Show it to them."

Now Iris stumbles. "Show us what?" The smirk on her flawless face cracks, and it makes my day.

Confidence returns to Mikahlo as he stands straighter.

"There's a distinct M-shaped chip on her upper right thigh. A mark I made!"

He plucks a magnifying glass and small mirror from my kit. "May I?" I nod my agreement, knowing what would come next. He hands me my tools, guiding me to the location on the statue. "It's small and hard to see at eye-level." He squats down and points to the site.

Pivoting the mirror, I see the small, yet distinct, chiseled mark I'd found before. "It's there. Just as described."

Iris looks stricken.

Gavin breaks his silence. "Forged replicas are one thing, Iris, but deception is quite another. Such fraud is a crime, both illegal and unethical." He limps to the door and gestures to it. "I must ask you to leave, ma'am."

"But the sculpture…"

"I hereby hold Aphrodite Immaculatus as evidence. Sue me if you want, but I imagine you'll have plenty of legal authorities to deal with soon enough, once I and any others you've defrauded come forward."

"Gavin…"

"I said leave. Now!"

She does so reluctantly, but her clenched fists and jaw tell the truth—she's been exposed and there's not a damn thing she can do about it. "Looks like Diogenes wins the day," I mutter.

Gavin shuts the door behind her and locks it. "She's been selling increasingly dubious works to gallerists and buyers for a while now. It's about time she's exposed."

It was quite the drama to witness, but it nags at me that I'm the only spectator in the room now. "Gavin, you sly devil. You already knew it was a fake."

"Theo, I owe you an apology and an explanation." He turns

to the corner to face one of the gallery cameras. "And I should document this in our recording as well." Gavin takes a deep breath and regards me with sad eyes. "I'm sorry that I couldn't tell you, but we needed your authentication to be unbiased."

"We?" I say, looking between Gavin and Mikahlo. "Did you two plan this as some sort of sting operation?"

"We did." Gavin says with a sheepish smile. "Iris sold me a piece last year that I later found questionable." He turns to Mikahlo, who picks up the thread.

"When visiting Gavin here, I saw her card on his desk. He showed me the work, a Greek terracotta figurine. Now I don't have your eye, Theo, but having been used before by Iris, I suspected she was up to her old tricks again."

Gavin nods. "Forgeries succeed because they satisfy our desires. And when Iris approached me with this Aphrodite, we hatched the plan to expose her."

"My friend, I have to admit, I was tempted to assert its authenticity, because the work was of impeccable quality. I really wanted it to be real." I roll to face Mikahlo. "It's an amazing reproduction. How did it come about?"

The young artist hangs his head. "I'm a bit ashamed to admit it. It was Iris's idea. I was still unknown and poor." He caresses the goddess with pure love and adoration. "And this dealer comes along offering me a chance to carve an actual Parian marble shard. I don't know how she got it, but who was I to question it? Sure, I needed the money, but for such a chance to pay homage to a true master. I couldn't say no."

"So, what happens to the Aphrodite?" I ask.

"Well, it's evidence for now," Mikahlo sighs. "But after that is said and done, Gavin plans to show it."

"Even though it's a fake?"

"Not fake," Gavin corrects me while pointedly admiring the Diogenes ring on his finger. "It's a reproduction. An homage from a modern master."

"And with the story of Iris's crimes as part of its provenance, every piece she commissioned will be worth a small fortune." I nod, impressed.

Behind Mikahlo, I swore I saw Cicero laughing.

PHYSICS NEWTON OVERLOOKED

by William Doreski

The four corners of this room
invite me to sit in all of them
at once. I do, and I feel more

angular than ever before.
The north corner smells of mice.
The south corner's too dark

to reveal its possible secrets.
The east corner expects me
to share the space with a god.

The west corner trembles with rain
festering from one tiny cloud.
I could gather my divided

attention and leave the room
but I sense a dynamic forming,
a physics Newton overlooked.

The room has no windows but

I see outside in all directions.
Someone's driving past with

a clatter of damaged gears.
Someone's sitting in a ditch
cuddling disembodied smiles.

A priest is mumbling to himself.
A dog wags but looks uncertain.
Direction and misdirection mate

and create a whole new person
and invite me to occupy
an otherwise vacant shell.

Hands on the Keyboard
by Diana Salas-Deitch

EAR

by Mona Leigh Rose

Constance turns the metronome dial up one notch, then another. Not enough for the tin-eared boy to notice. But enough to make his fingers work harder. His sticky, fat little fingers, smearing Cheeto dust and Mountain Dew on her pristine keys. Perhaps enough to make him whine over dinner to his helium-breasted cartoon of a mother until she shrieks, *You sniveling twit! You shame of my blood!* Her pitch rising until it shatters every flatscreen, rhinestone-crusted iPhone, and golden doodad they hold dear in their philistine little souls.

Does God still punish hubris in this way? He should.

The grandfather clock frees Constance with five peals, B flat. Her last lesson of the week has blessedly come to an end. She locks the door behind the boy, pulls the window shades. Wipes each piano key with a cloth diaper dipped in distilled water. Watches a cube of frozen lasagna turn in the microwave. She eats at the kitchen table, left hand in her lap, napkin at her right elbow, because she may be alone but is not a savage. Washes, dries, stacks her dish in the cupboard. Files the week away in a tidy mental folder labeled Good Riddance.

Constance allows the smallest of sighs to drift through her apartment.

At precisely 6:05 p.m., she walks to the Courthouse Sunken Gardens, folding chair under one arm, folded blanket over the other. She snakes her way through the languorous bodies stretched every which way across the grass, a modern-day Sodom and Gomorrah ripe for smiting. In front of the stage, she plants her chair in the center of her spread blanket. Folds her hands in her lap and waits for the program to begin.

"Ms. Potter?" A round-cheeked smile invades her line of sight. She retreats to the chair's furthest reaches. "I knew that was you," the invader says. "The second I saw the back of your head, I'm all, that's Ms. Potter."

"Mrs. Potter," Constance says.

"Do you remember me? Missy Adams. I took lessons, like, forever ago."

Missy Adams. Exquisite ear. Agile fingering. One of the few students in a dour parade of dullards who showed true promise. *Then.* Now, an intruder encroaching on her personal space. "Yes. Missy. How nice to see you." Constance pronounces each word in staccato, so there can be no mistake.

The body connected to the smile plants itself on Constance's blanket like an invited guest, bare legs and arms crossing the Scotch plaid at disconcerting angles. "Mrs. Potter. Who'd have thought?"

Constance reaches over her armrest to brush dirt off the blanket with exaggerated hand sweeps. "The program will start soon," she says, nodding toward the music stands posted like sentries on stage.

The oblivious thing has the nerve to smile. "I know,

right? I'm meeting friends for happy hour, but saw the sign and thought, that's what I need, a little music." Missy slips a knapsack off tan shoulders. "Weird thing is, I thought about you just yesterday."

Constance stops brushing. No one thinks of Constance. Not even Constance.

"I 3D printed a half-scale replica of a keyboard my freshman year. I take it out when I need to vent. If I'm cramming for a test, head full of quadratic equations, it really helps to—" She pounds her fingers on the blanket like a lunatic.

"One can't play a paper keyboard."

"Not paper, plastic. Looks totally legit."

"But not legitimate. Your little toy lacks hammers, dampers, strings. You can't possibly know if you're playing the piece correctly."

Purple-tipped hair haloes Missy's bright eyes. "That's the best part. I always nail it."

Constance fingers the wiry gray atop her own head. "Ridiculous."

"No, for real. The music takes me out of my head. Debussy if I'm anxious, Beethoven if I'm tired. Bach...well, everyone knows what Bach's for."

Constance studies the young face, the unguarded way Missy's lips part to reveal a gap between her front teeth. Regret hasn't found her yet. What need could she possibly have for Bach?

Missy pulls a juice carton from her knapsack. "I've got this gig in the uni's cognitive psych lab," she says, and takes a long swallow from the carton. "Grunt work, but looks good on grad school apps, plus I can study there after hours. I keep the keyboard in my desk." She wipes a bright pink drip from her chin.

The smell makes Constance dizzy. "Guava," she says.

"What?"

"Your juice."

"Right! My roomie buys it from this little market down in Ventura. Delish. Most people have never heard of it."

"My husband was stationed in Taiwan during the Vietnam War. We drank guava juice every morning."

Missy tips the carton toward her. "Sorry, you want some?"

Constance is surprised to find that she does. So much so that she pushes away thoughts of germs and viruses and body bags stacked on hospital loading docks, closes her eyes, and takes a long swallow from the soaked paper lips. A snippet of memory startles her with its clarity: The scent of fragrant white blossoms drifting through an open window. Children laughing from somewhere beyond the trees. Tom's hands caressing her shoulders while she plays, his kiss on her neck.

Constance twists in her chair until her knees nearly touch Missy's. "Yesterday."

"Hmm?"

"You said you thought about me yesterday."

"Right! I used the keyboard."

"Tell me, what did you play?"

Missy's cheeks flush. "Okay, but hear me out. I'm running this student volunteer through a test, ink blots, basic stuff. And he starts to cry. Like, buckets. And I'm all, holy crap, they're gonna fire my—" she shoots Constance a look "—fire me if I can't get this dude to stop crying. I pull out the keyboard and ask him his favorite song from when he was a kid, tell him to follow my fingers and hear the notes in his head. So..." she presses her hands over her eyes, peeks at Constance between

146

splayed fingers. "I played *Twinkle, Twinkle Little Star.*" She falls back on the blanket in a cloud of giggles.

"And?"

"And he stops crying. Sings, even. Said it made his week."

"No," Constance says, her voice too sharp, impatient for the answer to a question that feels strangely urgent. She softens her tone. "I meant, what made you think of *me?*"

"You gave me that gift. To make sense of the world through music."

"With a keyboard that doesn't play?"

"Not the notes. But it plays the music."

"Music no one can hear?"

"Music you hear in your heart."

The words float between them like a long-forgotten song. Music you hear in your heart. Constance reaches for the melody but it eludes her.

A microphone screeches. "Ladies and Gentlemen." A trio has materialized on stage. Missy reclines on the blanket, tucks an arm behind her head and closes her eyes. Constance turns in her chair until her knees point straight at the stage.

The violinist draws his bow. Bach's Air on a G String. Haunting when played well, deadly in capricious hands. Constance focuses on the composition. A sharp note raises the hair on her arms. She looks down at Missy, who doesn't stir, bliss shining from every pore. How does she do that? Constance squeezes her eyes shut and waits to feel something. The cello steps on the violin's opening. Her eyes pop open. This is ridiculous. She should just listen to the program the way she always—A note reaches beyond her ear, incongruous to the composition but warm and familiar. She rests her head against the chair back and allows her eyelids to drift closed. She hears a flute, but not the one on stage, the plastic kind you could buy at the Five and Dime when she was young, so young. Her small fingers pressed against the holes, the air from her lungs wringing joy out of noise. Grandma singing along. You are my sunshine…

The cello on stage joins the flute, warms into a voice. Tom's voice. I'll only be a month in-country, then retire at combat grade. It will mean more money. Julliard for you, med school for me. For a better future. He squeezed her hand. A beautiful future. And why shouldn't they have a beautiful future? A bright, glorious life was their birthright and destiny. She packed his footlocker, tucked in a note to make him blush when he reached for a fresh shirt. In the doorway, he knelt down to kiss her belly where it strained against the thin cotton dress. See you soon, little man, then made her laugh with a sharp salute to his unborn son. Certainly a son, because that's what they wished. When the grave-eyed Sargeant stood on her porch three weeks later with a folded flag in his outstretched hands, she couldn't fathom what it had to do with her. You've made a mistake, she said. He can't be dead. We have plans. She repeated the word plans like a sacred chant until the Sargeant's startled gaze swept down to her hand and Constance felt the shards of her shattered juice glass slicing into her palm. Later—a day, a week, a lifetime?—as her hands spasmed above the keyboard, aching with need, unable to play a single note, she felt the first bead of blood trickle down her thigh.

Applause jolts her upright. She sits alone on the blanket, the juice carton on its side next to her. A fragrant pink stain spreads like outstretched fingers across the blanket's tight weave.

148

LINGUISTIC RELATIVITY

by Stella Ho

Certain layers of reality
could be experienced by stringing
certain sounds together. A study
of certain gain and loss by speaking
one language instead of another.

My parents taught me to collect
words to get closer to the world.
I am always learning and forgetting,
crossing borders and returning to shore.

I like to lose myself in things completely.
It was the same with you.

Our midnight conversations
a study of longevity.
Which words stay
in our bones at daybreak?

I only remember:
a lexicon of the body,
a lexicon of the heart,
standing between a door and a door.

The Recycler
by Diana Salas-Deitch

THE RECYCLER

by Jeremy Gold

"Request denied," said Commander Jackson.

"But I'm the only crewmember in the whole section," Engineer First Class George Dally argued.

"And Lieutenant Chang is the only navigator. And Lieutenant Langley is the only pilot. And I'm the only XO. So get back to work."

"But you all have backups. What happens if I get..."

"Now! That was an order, engineer."

Langley blew him a kiss from her seat on the command bridge. Chang snickered and shook his head, but didn't bother to turn around. George saw his reflection on the screen, stretching the width of the bridge. A large asteroid field filled the upper right quadrant. He'd only been on the command deck twice before, both times when the ship was moored at Aries Station for repairs.

"And Dally?" Jackson said.

"Yes, sir."

"Shower and wash that god-damned, filthy uniform before you ever set foot on my bridge again."

"Yes, sir." George turned and left.

***

He slumped down on the bench and closed his eyes as the internal transportation system, ITS-pod, snaked through the huge vessel. For the third time that year, the XO of the New Holland had denied him a pay raise and had refused to hire a second crewman in Recycling. Unbelievable! Without a waste management engineer, there would be no recycling. And without recycling, there would be no space travel. His job was as important as any on the whole ship! Traveling through space without a backup was insane.

He wasn't some raw recruit. He was a fully trained engineer with degrees from the Academy in Recycling and Spacefaring Propulsion. He'd interned on the Aries for two years, and apprenticed for another two on the Hammerstein, before Vega Tours hired him to take over Recycling on the New Holland. Three years he'd worked on this ship! And in all that time, he'd received one, two-credit raise. Two credits! Two credits wouldn't buy him a used comic vid.

Not only did he handle all of the ship's recycling, but he filled in for Jenkins when he was too drunk to manage the engines. And only a month ago, he'd helped Kowalski overhaul the whole air filtration system—all by themselves.

Back on Singletary Station, before he'd gone off to school, he and his dad had handled all the machinery for the whole base. Granted, it wasn't a big station; less than two hundred full-time inhabitants lived there. But he and his dad had done it all. They'd kept the whole thing afloat.

Until his dad had lost his legs when that reactor blew, which easily could have been avoided had their requisition for a new shield been approved. But like all the outfits he'd worked for, he'd been told to "make do," or "we just don't have the funds," or "just make it go right!"

The pod swooshed to its final stop—well off the beaten path of the paying public—and the doors hissed open. Crew members never ventured down to Recycling, either. Long ago, George had grown accustomed to the smell of rotting food and human waste. Not so, the majority of other human noses.

On his way to his office—the closet-sized control room—George stopped and checked the gauge on the side of tank one. Oxygen and carbon dioxide levels were all normal. He moved on to tank two. Water level at ninety percent. He put his ear up against the cold stainless steel of tanks three, four, and five, listening to the gurgling sound and gentle vibrations of trillions of microscopic organisms breaking down human waste into their component elements. Everything looked and sounded normal.

Back in his office, he pulled up the maintenance schedule. Everything was green except for a single, flashing red box halfway down the screen. The filters on tank five were at nineteen percent and needed swapping out. He transferred all flow to tanks three and four before shutting down number five and ambling over to the tool locker. He grabbed his tool belt, a carton of new filters, and went to work.

Masks and gloves helped, but there was no way around the stench of sludge. Cleaning tanks and swapping out dirty filters was foul and nasty work, and no amount of protection ever completely negated the smell. George knelt, pulled a spanner from his belt, and slipped it over the first nut.

Scrubbing out a single tank and switching out the filters

took about five hours—with two people on the job, less than half that time. But there weren't two people on the job. There was just one, George Dally. Vega Tours, in their infinite wisdom, had decided that one waste management engineer was sufficient for a Europa-class vessel—was adequate to meet the needs of two hundred sixteen passengers and forty-seven crew members on a month-long tour of Sector Sixteen of the Milky Way.

Cleaning tanks was not only tedious and smelly work, it was hard on the back. It also gave one a lot of time to think. His recent foray onto the bridge occupied most of his thoughts: Commander Jackson, standing smugly in front of his command chair, denying his request; his two condescending lieutenants, Chang and Langley, smirking and blowing kisses, as if he was some kind of lesser human being. Which amongst the crew… let's face it, he was.

Lieutenant Kaur was the only one who'd ever acknowledged his existence. Just last week, on the way to the mess hall, she'd asked him how his day was going. And then stood there in the passageway, waiting, as if she'd really wanted to know. He'd stared into her eyes—deep brown with flecks of yellow—not knowing what to say. Until she'd smiled and shrugged her shoulders and he'd uttered, "Ah, okay, I guess." And then she'd asked if he'd seen that new movie about that kid with the supernatural powers. And he'd said, "No, not yet." And she said, "It's supposed to be really good." And he'd nodded. And finally, she'd said she had to get going. And he'd said, "Me too." And she walked back toward Medical, and he turned and trudged back to Recycling.

If ever a caste system existed on a ship, the waste management engineer occupied the lowest class. Despite all the sensory safeguards, nobody wanted anything to do with anyone who dealt with piss and shit all day long—and often, long into the night. Lonely was the life of a man who dealt in human waste for a living.

Just a month ago, George had overheard others talking in the mess hall about what engineers on the ship earned. Not only were those who worked in the bowels of ships looked down upon, they were poorly paid.

Not having an assistant or a junior—anyone who could fill his shoes should something happen to him—was reckless. Suppose he got sick or became incapacitated—like Dad—the New Holland was screwed. If the ship was lucky, it might be able to reach some kind of station before everyone expired. Given the vastness of space, though, the odds weren't great.

Captains were supposed to know everything about the posts under their command. Captain Manseau, though? The two times he'd visited Recycling, he hadn't had a clue what was going on and couldn't wait to leave. All George's attempts at meeting with him to discuss his situation had been met with, "Talk to the XO."

George's job was vitally important! No recycling meant no fresh air or water. Which quickly led to no air or water of any kind—period. This quickly resulted in death. Everyone knew that. If they didn't, they were idiots.

He finally tightened the last nut, slipped the spanner back in his tool belt, wiped his greasy hands down the legs of his coveralls, and rose to his feet. His back told him to report to sick bay. His mind told him to lie down on the cot behind tank one. The cot was closer.

Two minutes later, he was dreaming of rescuing Lieutenant Kaur from a band of Kantana traffickers.

***

George raised his head and cracked his eyelids. The normal

The Recycler / Gold   **155**

purr of the ship sounded slightly off. He placed a hand on the bulkhead wall behind his head, feeling for the usual vibrations of the engines two partitions away. Given their coordinates, the New Holland shouldn't have been so quiet. Except for that asteroid field, there was nothing out here to warrant shutting down the main engines. Shutting down the engines on a Europa-class vessel was a serious undertaking. Something was not right. Something was wrong.

He swung his legs off the cot, strode over to his office, and called up the main screen. All readouts were within acceptable limits. He double-checked tank five, the one he'd just cleaned. According to the display, it was operating at ninety-eight percent. Just to make sure, he walked over to the tank, put a hand against the cold metal, and glanced at its gauge. Everything was good. At least in Recycling, everything was running smoothly. Shutting down the engines had nothing to do with waste management.

Thirty seconds later, a burst of static sounded from the ship's communication system, followed by the voice of the captain.

"To all passengers and crew, this is your captain. Everything is fine. Do not be alarmed. There is nothing to worry about."

Instantly, George was alarmed and worried.

"Your captain was right to tell you everything is fine and not to be alarmed," said another, more gravelly voice. "If everyone cooperates and does exactly what I say, everything will be okay."

The voice paused, allowing the warning to register fully.

"I am Captain Anton Jerrod," continued the new voice. "And I am now in command of the New Holland. Do not be alarmed. Do as I say, and nobody will get hurt."

"Oh, shit. Pirates!" muttered George. They must have been

waiting in ambush in the asteroid field. A moment later, his suspicions were confirmed.

"I'm not an unkind man," Jerrod said. "I mean none of you any harm. I am a simple man involved in the business of wealth redistribution."

In other words, a pirate, George thought.

"All passengers will return to their rooms," Jerrod continued. "Leave your doors open. Those who don't will be dealt with severely.

"As for the crew—and I have a readout of the complete, forty-seven-man roster—report to the main cargo bay, immediately. Anyone trying to send a distress signal will be spaced. Anyone trying to resist will be spaced. Anyone not doing exactly as I say will be spaced. If all forty-seven crew don't show up, I will begin spacing the ones who have. Passengers and crew, you have five minutes to get to your respective stations. Do not be late. I have men standing by at all the airlocks. Jerrod out."

A Europa-class ship was a very large vessel, and George would have to hustle to reach the cargo bay within the allotted five minutes—especially with all the passengers and crew using the ITS at the same time. He wiped his hands on his overalls—more out of habit than because they were overly dirty—and took off down the passageway.

"Come on, come on, come on," he muttered, shifting from foot to foot. According to the screen above the doors, the next pod would arrive in four minutes.

The pod arrived at the posted time, the doors swished open, and George stepped aboard. All eight seats were empty. "Cargo bay," he said.

George would explain that getting from Recycling to the main cargo bay in five minutes was impossible—especially with all the passengers and crew using the system at the same time. Jerrod would understand. He wouldn't really start executing crewmembers if one man was late, would he? On the other hand, the man was a pirate. And pirates executed people. Because that's what they did. Because they were pirates. And pirates weren't keen on insubordination. Or at leaving witnesses.

The easiest way to eliminate everyone in one fell swoop would be to blow up the ship after taking everything of value. No... They wouldn't destroy the whole ship. A ship this size was worth too much—the salvage value of the hull alone was worth billions. They'd space everyone and keep the ship. Tow it to some pirate hideout on the other side of the galaxy and strip it clean. That's what George would have done.

The shuttle stopped and the doors slid open. According to the station clock, he was already three minutes late. He ran down the short passage to the cargo bay and burst inside. Except for Captain Manseau, all the crew were lined up down the center of the bay. The captain knelt before Jerrod. The pirate had a gun to his head.

Pirates were swarming over the ship's four shuttle craft, uncoupling moorings, and getting them ready for departure. Other pirates were hurrying up ramps, loading the small tour boats with bags and boxes of loot. All carried multiple weapons clipped to armored vests.

Jerrod looked up from Captain Manseau and smiled. "Ah... Number forty-seven. So glad you could join us. I was just about to put a bullet in your captain's head." He gestured to the crew with his gun. "Line up with the others."

"I'm really, really sorry. I got here as fast as I could," George panted. "I work on the far end of the ship. And the ITS takes at least...”

“Stop,” Jerrod ordered.

George stopped talking and jogged in his ungainly shuffle to the end of the line. He bent over and put his hands on his knees. Not since cadet school had he exercised as much. Jerrod lifted the captain by his epaulets and shoved him toward the line. George didn’t know if pirate captains had commanders or XOs, but Jerrod turned and said something to a man standing next to him. The large man nodded, raised a pad, and ran a finger down the screen. A few seconds later, he stopped and handed it off to Jerrod.

Jerrod studied the screen for a minute before walking forward and stopping two meters in front of the line of crewmembers. He was a tall man. Handsome, with neatly-combed dark hair. Strong jaw. No visible scars. No eyepatch. Not your everyday, stereotypical, nightmarish-looking pirate captain. The two, rougher-looking men on either side of him held rifles—big rifles—the kind that eliminated players from the game without the need of expert marksmanship.

“Okay, let’s see what we have here,” Jerrod said to the crew. His gaze stopped at the end of the line. “You, Mr. Late Man,” he said to George. “Step forward.”

George straightened up. “Me?”

A corner of Jerrod’s mouth rose a couple of centimeters. “You work in recycling, yes?” The pirate glanced at the pad again. “George Dally?”

“Ah...yeah.”

“I can tell by your uniform. How many work in your section?”

“In recycling? In waste management?”

The pirate chuckled. “Yes. Waste management. How

many?"

"Uh...just me."

Jerrod pointed his gun at the captain. "Is this true? On a ship this size?"

The captain nodded. "Vega Tours runs a fiscally sound ship."

Jerrod shook his head. "Fools."

George stared at a spot of grease on his sleeve.

"Our own engineer had a falling out with us...and we had to let him go," Jerrod continued. "So unfortunate."

His two bodyguards snickered.

Jerrod took a few steps toward George. "How much do they pay you?"

George told him.

"What's your training? Start at the beginning. Tell me everything you do."

George told him, starting with growing up on Singletary Station.

Jerrod laughed. "A man of your training and importance? That's what they're paying you? Are they serious?"

George stared straight ahead. Frozen. Too scared to say anything, terrified that any second, Jerrod would raise his gun and blow him away—to intimidate the rest of the crew and show them he meant business. Because Jerrod was a pirate. And that's what pirates did. And George was a nobody.

Instead, the pirate extended a hand and said, "Welcome to my crew...Chief."

George gasped, then leaned forward and glanced down the line, stopping on Lieutenant Kaur. "Ah...I'll need an assistant," he said.

THE CONDO WILL BE EMPTIED

by Wendy Jean MacLean

She clears the closets
at high noon.
Her sight is perfect.
She sorts and bags
old shirts, old ties
and clears the space
with wisdom and grace.

My sight is dim
when I arrive
at Compline. I hear
chants and prayers
from every shoe.
Every pillowcase
has its own supplication
as I try to discern
what to keep
and what to let go.

Eventually
the condo will be emptied
of the remnants
of sweaters and scarves

stories and prayers.
The light will stream
through bare windows
onto sills bereft
of treasures and plants.
The fridge will hum
Vespers and Lauds.

What is left
after everything
has been given away?
Dawn and dusk
come and go.
Ghosts appear
from time to time
at Happy Hour.
They bring the wine
to toast their children
as they savor eternity
together.
Well done
good and faithful servants.
Twelve bags for the Salvation Army.

MIDNIGHT ENTOMOLOGIST

by Veronica Tucker

Each night, I step into the field
with a notebook, a net, and no intention
of catching anything.
It's the light I'm after.
Some beetles carry it inside them,
flickers under hard-backed armor,
small engines of glow.
I squat low in the grass,
quiet as a thought half-formed,
and watch them rise.
To name something is not to know it.
Still, I whisper Linnaean spells:
Photinus pyralis, Elateridae,
incantations to keep the silence
from caving in.
There are so many ways to measure night:
by temperature, by moon shape,
by the number of wings that brush your wrist
before you feel alone again.
Once, I thought I saw a signal.
Three long flashes, a pause,
then two short bursts.
A code? A prayer? A warning?

I recorded it anyway.
The sky does not always explain itself.
By dawn, the grass is wet
with more than dew.
The pages curl in my hand.
No one waits for this data.
Still, I go.
Still, I watch.
Still, I try
to count the light.

SHOWER THOUGHTS

by Chynna Foster

This morning in the shower
I paid attention to all the places I'd been bruised.
Intergalactic narrative taking harvest in my skin
My feet were cracked with highways
Some I'd walked,
Some I'd only dreamed of.
The edges of my toenails carved chemtrails through pink
    skin
I hadn't noticed.

When I got out, I paid attention too
For the first time attending to each drop of water
With a fresh towel (a delicacy!)
Put tender hands to work (my hands).
I had the thoughts:
Well this is boring
Why do people bother?

But I noticed the rhythm slowing,
 Rib cage expanding,
 Voices quiet—
Then thought
Sometimes this is alchemy.

Oregon Snow
by Diana Salas-Deitch

OREGON SNOW

by Kirby Michael Wright

A truck with Oregon plates arrives in San Diego at dusk. When the driver slides open the cargo door, his Christmas trees are coated with lumps of snow and sheets of ice. There's so much white he imagines an artificial forest smothered in flocking spray.

"How'd this happen?" asks Home Depot man.

The driver tucks his hands in the kangaroo pocket of his sweatshirt. "Forgot to close that damn vent," he mutters.

He climbs on the bumper, grabs a chain hanging from the roof, and swings up. He shakes branches—white tumbles onto the steel bed. He kicks and shovels snow and ice into the parking lot. A mogul forms. Kids gather. Most are boys, but there are twin sisters. They grab the cold and shape without gloves. Snowballs sail through the half-light and splatter on asphalt. A few fathers join in. One father under-hands a snowball that bounces off his wife's head.

"Wanna play rough, eh?" she giggles and retaliates with ice.

The driver enjoys this unexpected winter. A boy leaps over the mogul, and others follow. The snow and ice don't seem to melt. The driver's happy his vent was open as he churned through the passes north of Eugene. The evergreen smell reminds him of home. He feels like a boy again.

YOU HEAR MY CALL

by Valerie Girard

The golden light reflects off your tawny breast,
Glimmering in the soft wave of the treetop branches
As the canyon blusters spurts of tingling breeze, then wind,
Promising wildness tonight.

Earlier, I quietly asked for your presence.
On this eve's half-moon rise,
To perch on the guardian's post that sways high
With the fluctuations of the canyon's breath.

No expectations, please,
It is not allowed in this reflection of the One
Just a humble request amidst
The rustling of long leaves as they crackle and wave
To their cohorts across the canyon.

You, Hawk, are my Spirit ally.
I look to you for confirmation
That I am able to connect to the Field.
Listen: I honor your presence with
Sweet murmuring, hopeful you feel the love,
Rejoicing that you would answer my call
With the penetrating gaze of your silence.

THE WERE-ALBATROSS'S SOLILOQUY

by Veronica Tucker

When the moon pulls taut across the sea
and the wind sharpens its teeth,
I forget the names they gave me.
Man. Monster. Mistake.
I fly.
Not as escape,
but as inheritance.
No one teaches you
how to land
when your feet forget the rhythm of ground.
Waves are easier than sidewalks.
Salt more forgiving than speech.
I've known the soft weight of feathers
and the ache of returning.
The hunger that does not live in the belly
but in the chest,
where memories molt
and regrow in strange colors.
There is no cage
like a closet full of shoes.
No trap
like a name sewn into clothing

that no longer fits.
Once, I flew so far
the sky forgot to end.
I counted stars until I ran out of numbers,
then made new ones.
When I came back,
they asked if I was cured.
I said nothing.
They would not understand
how the horizon spoke to me,
how silence felt like kin.
I am not asking for love.
Only wind.
Only space.
Only to shed the human long enough
to feel the sky
for what it is:
a mirror too vast
to break.

Grace Eternal
by Diana Salas-Deitch

172

GRACE ETERNAL

by Nicholas Deitch

In a city, on the Westside, in the old Washington Hotel, a woman sat at her darkened window with the sash open wide, and let the warm night air wash over her, tinged with a fine mist of rain that tickled her arm at rest on the sill. To see her from the street, one might puzzle at the woman who sat in the dark gazing out across the night. One might even think to wave, though such an effort would go unnoticed.

Her vision clouded since birth, Grace did not come easily to sleep. The night was too comfortable in the spattered orbs of color and light that illumined her world. The sounds of the restless street below, tires on wet pavement, footfalls of hard-heeled shoes, the buzz and sputter of tired neon. Light and sound and color enfolded Grace in an amniotic calm that those blessed with sight could not fully comprehend.

She sat in the quiet and listened. Muffled voices through the walls, an argument, a moan of ecstasy, a man sobbing as a woman chastised. The tromping lumber of vanilla guy in the apartment above, whose passing in the hall smelled faintly of cake. Grace knew them, their comings and goings and wantings and pains. Their scents, their habits and much of their fears, and their lusts.

A small thump on the bed. A cat stepped into her lap with a motored purr and pressed its head to her hand.

"Hungry, Freddy?" She scritched a furry head. "Of course you are." She set the cat on the floor and stood to make her way across the small apartment. At the cupboard she reached for a pouch of cat food, but found none.

"I'm sorry, Fredrick. I forgot to get your food." She went to the nightstand and felt for the clock and pressed the button. A synthesized voice announced the time, 9:22 pm.

She bent and reached for the cat, now wrapping itself around her legs. "I'll step out to the market for just a moment." She patted a furry head. "I'll say hi to Earl for you, ok, Freddy?"

At her closet, Grace found a shawl and wrapped it around her shoulders. She went to the door and felt for the key that hung on a hook by the jamb. She flipped a switch and her apartment filled with milky light and familiar shadows. "I won't leave you in the dark, Freddy." She bent to give the cat one more scritch, grabbed a shopping bag folded by the door and then stepped out of her little apartment and into the passage she knew by rote.

Grace walked down the corridor, letting her hand trail along the wainscot. She passed the door of Mrs. Khosla, chipped paint on wood. The murmurings of a television within, and the lingering aromas of curry and garlic. At the stairs she felt for the rail and began the careful descent, one step at a time, into the darkness.

The small lobby was quiet, lit only by a single incandescent sconce above the mailboxes, and the light of a streetlamp outside. On the last few steps Grace caught the scent, the smell like soured milk and sweat.

"Hello?" She spoke into the darkness, toward the sound of shallowed breaths. At the base of the stairs she scanned the walls looking for unfamiliar shapes in the murky light. The scent grew stronger, the breathing stopped.

She called again, "Hello? I don't think I know you. Do you need help?"

A dark shape retreated further into the shadows. A slow exhale of tentative breath. "Why do you stare at me?" The voice of a man, weak and uncertain, Grace could hear him trembling.

"What do you mean?" She stepped back. "Who are you?"

"From your window, you stare at me. Every night, you sit there and stare." The voice swayed, fingers tapping at keys in the pocket of his pants.

Grace reached for the railing. "No, I don't. I like the night, and I can't—"

"I see you, Grace Tillerman. I see you watching me. God sent you to find me." The shadow wavered, and swallowed. "When will it happen?"

"When will what happen?" Grace puzzled at the strange intruder, dark and still, reeking of fear. "And how do you know my name?"

"In my dreams you come to me. You speak to me from the mouth of God, that he will bring me to damnation for the ruin I've caused. And I—" Swallowing tears. "Please, ask him to forgive me."

"You need help. You need to leave me alone." Grace stepped toward the door.

The shadow came forward, a hand grabbed her arm. "I do need help. Yes, yes. Please, Grace. Help me. I'm an angel, too.

Don't you see? But I fell. I know it. I fell so low that God can't hear me through his rage. Tell him I'm sorry. Tell him I want to live." His grip tightened.

"Leave me alone." Grace pulled away and pushed herself out the door, onto the stoop, down to the familiarity of the nighttime street. She turned to walk toward the small market, more quickly than usual, her trembling hand trailing along the low wall. The sidewalk wet with splashes of color, her face tingled in the evening mist. The smell of the rain-washed street. The sound of music from an open window. A dog barking down an alley.

The scuff of footsteps from behind. She turned back and stared into the darkness. Out of the murk a shadow pushed past her, the grunt of a man, not so clean, the stink of a cigarette in his wake.

Grace exhaled. Forty more strides and she stopped again to listen through her beating heart. A horn sounded somewhere, long and insistent. Grace took a deep breath and stepped into the blooming halo of a reddish neon glow, Samuel's Royal Market.

The door chimed her arrival, the air thick with offerings, of spearmint and burnt coffee and hot dogs turning too long on an electric spit. A fan wobbled above, the place awash in jibbering fluorescence.

"Hey, Gracie." The night guy, Earl, a shadow behind the counter, the glow of a small TV.

Grace passed him, then stopped and faced the counter. "Freddy says 'hi,' Earl. He's hungry, and I forgot to buy his food this morning."

"No worries." A smile in his voice. "That's why I sit on this stool 'til midnight. So Freddy won't go hungry."

She nodded, and walked down the aisle toward the hum of the coolers and stopped halfway. She felt for the foil pouches of Kitty Buffet, Freddy's favorite. The door chimed again and Grace heard Earl's greeting, and the scuff of shoes that turned down her aisle, stopped, stepped back, then turned to go down the next.

Footsteps to the coolers, and the sucking sound of a door pulled open. The clink of bottles from a rack and the thunk of the door as it closed. Someone passed her, the man on the street? The stink of stale cigarettes.

Grace put six pouches of Kitty Buffet into her bag, and walked to the front, the smell of the man still standing there.

The register rang, and Earl's voice replied, "That's eight-twenty-seven, my man." The chink of the cash drawer sliding open. She heard Earl gasp.

"Empty it. All of it, in the bag, or I'll splatter your brains all over the wall."

"Ok, ok. Don't shoot me, man."

"What are you looking at, bitch?" A hand came hard across her face, Grace stumbled back, her breath caught in her throat.

"Don't hurt her!" Earl's voice, shouting. "She can't even—"

A gunshot, and the sound of someone gasping, falling down.

"Earl?" Grace called out.

The door flew open in a rush of chimes and shadow. "Grace, get down!"

She fell to her knees. The humph of bodies colliding, bottles smashing and shattered glass, a gunshot, and the thud of someone hitting the floor. The door rang open and then wooshed closed.

The fan wobbled above. The rotisserie turned. Grace on her

knees, her limbs shaking, her breath cut short. A low moaning on the floor before her, a voice strained. "Grace…"

She shuffled forward, through spilt beer and shards of glass, and felt a hand, a sleeve, his chest. The smell of soured milk and sweat, his shirt damp and sticky.

She touched his face, his breathing shallow through her fingers.

"Grace…" His voice thin. "You're an angel, Grace. You may not know it, but you're an angel of God."

"Shhh." She lifted him and pulled him to herself.

"Tell God I'm sorry, Grace. Please, tell God I want to live."

"Quiet now." She stroked his hair. "It's time to go home."

IS IT LIKE BEING LOST

by Naomi Bess Leimsider

because I know what that's like.
When it's late,
and I walk the wrong way down the wrong street again.
When I lay it down,
give it up, there and nowhere and here and disappear,
where will I be?

I go looking for you, but I need a mind
not like mine,
with its severe lack of cognitive maps, perception,
directions.
I should be taken out
back, buried under street signs, way under the framework
of the
familiar yet unfamiliar
grid. When you don't know where you are, you lose your
body.
Three-dimensional patterns
appear flattened, the universe's rules upended. Upside
down,
trying to go back
the way I came, but always in the wrong direction.

People's ideas about how to fix the problem
                    don't address what to do
with the bits and pieces, frayed fragments, of my brain's
        scattered
                            debris. So little ability
to balance, calibrate distance, that one day I'll slide off the
        wrong side
            of the familiar yet unfamiliar
grid, on the wrong block, on the wrong street, in the
        wrong home.
                        And then I won't live
anywhere anymore.

You always knew where you were,
                        where you were going,
but I still tell people you are lost as explanation. Did you
        know it
            instantly? I know the way
you can suddenly know you are not in the right place.
        Until now,
                        you haven't known
what it's like to be counted among the missing, that other
        people's ideas
            about how to fix the problem
leave you abandoned, stranded, in the wrong spaces,
        calling in from
                            remote places,

where search parties can't locate any signs of life or be
  seen.

More often than not,
        it's late, and I am still somewhere,
but I can't see what's ahead of me. When you don't know
            where you are,
you lose your body. How will I let go, like you, transition
  from
        tethered to untethered
on this familiar yet unfamiliar grid. When I walk the
  wrong way
            down the wrong street,
lay it down there and nowhere and here and disappear.
      When I give it up, where will I be?

Red Rocks
by Diana Salas-Deitch

RED ROCKS

by Zach Keali'i Murphy

It'd been seven years to the day since Rod and Miriam found out that their son, Will, had died during a hiking trip in Sedona. He'd fallen into a crevice, snapped his neck. His body was found a few weeks later.

The living room was quiet and drab. A thin ray of sunrise pierced through an opening in the curtains, illuminating a flurry of dust particles in the air. Rod was in the kitchen starting up the coffee machine. Miriam walked into the living room and took a dust cloth to the coffee table. "I'll have mine iced today," she said. "This dry heat is enough to make a fountain feel parched."

"It's a hot one," Rod said as he opened the freezer door. He squinted his eyes at a full tray of ice cubes as the chilled air graced his pockmarked face. "I think I'll do the same," he said.

Rod prepared the iced coffee, walked into the living room, placed the two glasses on a pair of coasters, and sat next to

Miriam on the couch. He grabbed the TV remote and pointed it toward the TV.

"What are you doing?" Miriam asked.

"What do you mean, what am I doing?" Rod answered. "I'm turning on the television set."

"We agreed not to turn on the news on this day," Miriam said.

Rod dropped the remote between the crack of the couch cushions. "Oh my gosh," he said. "How did I not realize?" He launched up from the couch, dashed to the kitchen, and traced his finger over the flower-themed calendar on the refrigerator. "August fifteenth," he said. He turned around toward Miriam. "Am I awful for forgetting?" he asked.

Miriam shook her head. "You haven't forgotten our son," she said. "Just the date when we found out. It must have slipped your mind."

Rod walked back into the living room and sat back down on the couch. "Miriam, I have to tell you something," he said.

"What's that?" Miriam asked.

"A couple of autumns ago, when I went golfing with Joe Tamburello," he said. "I didn't go golfing."

"What are you trying to tell me?" Miriam asked.

"I went to Red Rock to see the spot where it happened."

Miriam set her coffee down on the table. "I knew something was peculiar that day," she said. "Whenever you go golfing, you always spend the rest of the night talking about eagles and birdies and hawks and whatever else type of scores you make in that game." Miriam ran her hands through her wavy, grey hair. "Why did you keep it a secret?" she asked.

"Because I knew it would upset you," Rod said.

"Well, that's no reason to keep a secret," Miriam said.

184

"I wanted to see what he saw," Rod said.

Miriam took a deep breath. "What was it like?" she asked.

"It was a beautiful view, Miriam," Rod said. "The most beautiful view." His eyes widened. "The rock formations were like works of art. Miles and miles of them. And the shades of red were like none I've ever seen before. It was as if God himself painted them."

"Wow," Miriam said.

"But what struck me the most," Rod said. "What struck me most is how short the fall was. It wasn't a long way down. Maybe five, six feet. It must have happened so fast."

Rod took a sip of his coffee. "He probably didn't even feel anything," he said.

"You're right," Miriam said. "Probably didn't even feel anything."

Rod and Miriam sat in silence for several minutes and stared into the blackness of the idle TV.

"Hell of a view," Rod said.

AFTER MY MOTHER DIED, I MADE PRANK CALLS

by Eddi Salado

From somewhere in the vast
delicate pages of the phonebook
I found the word "Love."
Pages and pages of Love.

After school I would sit
crossed-legged on my bedroom
floor and call Love,
then wait in silence
as the tiny voice
replied, "Hello, Hello?"
"Is anyone there?"

I pictured children
at a table where she
had baked a cake,
or made stacks of pancakes,
warm and fragrant.
maple syrup
sticky on the table,

and Mrs. Love
in the kitchen with
the clunky receiver
pressed against her pale cheek,
creases in her pretty
forehead—wondering why
there is only a hush

on the other end—
only the sound
that longing makes.

Fever Dream
by Diana Salas-Deitch

FACEBOOK NECROPOLIS

by Jenny Burman

You ask what we did all those nights in January? Picture this—
we drank Diet Pepsi, because Dan no longer drank, and we
stayed up telling stories. We scrolled. We weren't physically
underground, but we were underground all the same, hiding
out from Dan's wife and all the people in Madison who knew
us. Never mind they were all so many miles away.

Dan had blackout maroon curtains and a large round diner
clock with green neon. Facebook was about ten years old. This
was before the great migration to Instagram, a movement that
would leave us behind. Social media platforms, like cemeteries,
go out of style, get too crowded. The clock read just after one
a.m.

Outside, the surf pounded. It sounded like the highway.
You ask what the highway sounds like. It sounds like a pulsing
artery, blood flowing at great speed: advance, retreat. Breathe
in, breathe out. The Jersey shore has a particular kind of pulse,

slightly evil.

"It's the afterlife in here," Dan said one night, as a wave crashed on the beach.

For a moment I thought he meant the room where we were holed up, his bedroom. It would have made sense, the way we were alone and telling our life stories, as though our lives were finished products—we'd done all our living. As though hiding out wasn't living.

He meant *Facebook* was the afterlife.

We lay on Dan's bed, naked, Dan's laptop open at the end of the bed.

"It used to be people faded away and you never heard a word about what city they lived in, whether they had kids," he said. "Now you can go into this—" he hesitated, looking for the word. "Into this *museum* and see who they married, what they look like at fifty-three." He held one finger in the air, more to say. "After fifty-three they stop posting pictures. They're still posting, showing you the vacations, but their bodies are—" he closed his hands into fists and exploded them. "Gone."

I shook my head. "It's like the afterlife, but only at one particular point in time," I said, and Dan gave me a dark look. "Only for one moment," I continued. "Things keep on, I mean," I pointed to the screen where a silver-haired man, a friend of Dan's, presumably younger than fifty-three, stood in front of a zinc bar with a hamburger in each hand, a severe look on his face. "That's probably not the last thing he'll ever post."

"I disagree!" Dan erupted, turning over and facing me. "It goddamn may well be the last thing he posts!" He rolled away from me. Getting out of bed, he hunted for his boxers. "God knows he could be breathing his last breath this very second. And then—" Dan gestured, palm up, at the screen. "That's the last thing he ever posted. Two hamburgers. Which one is he gonna eat first? The last thing he ever said. His gravestone will be somber but the last thing he said on here was something about two hamburgers!"

"Have I offended you?"

He pulled on his khakis. Then a T-shirt with thin, brown horizontal stripes over cream, like something a ten-year-old boy would wear.

Dressed now, he lay back down—the laptop open at the end of the bed—moved closer to me and I thought he was going to put his arm around my waist. But he put hands on the laptop keyboard and started scrolling.

"Look at this!" he said, stopping the scroll at a user whose avatar was a mean-looking tabby cat. A string of happy birthdays at the top of his feed. "Dead! This dude has been in the ground for two years! And look at all these people wishing him happy birthday—two weeks ago!"

"*Dear Nathaniel,*" Dan read. "*You are missed. Happy birthday and sweet dreams, Prince.*"

He scrolled to another dead friend. "See? It's a necropolis in here!"

Was it worth pointing out that a necropolis was not the afterlife? I decided not.

***

It became a game. The dead became our entertainment, along with the pre-dead, as we called our surviving Facebook friends.

For five or six nights, surf pounding, we searched Dan's friends, and he told their stories, or sometimes we collaborated and made up their fates, laughing, talking, our words falling to bits in the air.

"That one, he's going to die in a Price Chopper parking lot.

The old woman he cut off in the express line is going to ram her cart into his backside. *Oh, I'm so sorry! Oh! You've fallen! Someone call 911!*"

"It's all so sad," Dan said, one night. "People are so sad." He stood and paced. We'd been meeting here on and off for about a year.

Outside of Facebook, Dan and I shared just a few friends. Carl was one. Dan trusted Carl. Carl didn't judge Dan for living separately from his wife. The three of us went out to dinner now and then. Or to the movies. One time I looked up from the table at the Thai/Korean restaurant in town and Carl was looking at me intently. I returned his gaze, and he shook his head. *What the hell!* I wanted to ask, *does this head shake mean? Was he judging me, even as he didn't judge Dan? Feeling sorry for me? What did he know?*

Dan sat on the bed hard enough to make the mattress bounce and put his hand on my hip and pulled the striped T-shirt over his head. All night, that shirt had been going over his shoulders in one direction or another.

"Let me tell you something," he said. "The trick to writing about people you know," he paused, aiming the balled-up shirt at the chair in front of his desk, but missed. It landed on the keyboard of his iMac. The trick to writing about people one knew, he continued, was to mix up all the real-life details so no one can ever be sure you're writing about them. I didn't need to be told this, but those words ring in my head now as I read story after story of his about women the protagonists hated and loved. None of it is about me. He wrote from his life, but everything he ever wrote about happened before we met. For me it was a different story, of course, because I was just starting out.

192

After Dan went back to Wisconsin, he told people I was a psycho bitch, because, he said, I had been telling people about our affair. Which was true. I told everyone all about it. That changed everything. He said I had given him no choice but to go back. Which he was probably planning to do anyway; I knew how this was going to end up from the start. Or I thought I did. Call it a lack of imagination. I could imagine only the most predictable outcome.

Another thing he told me. He liked to keep people off balance. Keep them guessing about where they stood with him. "Everyone except you," he said. But that would change.

On our last night in New Jersey, he held me and said, "we wasted our time together, Lou." I realize now it was our best moment.

I learned of his death on Facebook. One day I thought of him—this was several years after that last embrace. He used to call me once or twice a year—ranting about how he'd cut his index finger on a can opener or had to have a salivary gland removed—and it had been a while since I'd heard from him. As I did every now and then, I opened his Facebook page to see if there were any new photos. Or new posts. On this day there were a lot of new photos. I knew right away. That's the first thing they do when someone dies, post pictures to stake their claim to the history.

His last breath had been a day earlier. A short while later, there were funeral arrangements. His son wrote, "anyone can come." Not that I would have gone. I have no business in Madison.

You ask what was the last thing he actually posted, his final statement? It was a picture of himself gazing mildly—not Dan-like at all—into the camera and the caption *WTF?*

A few years later, I figured out how to write about Dan. I pretended we had not frittered away all those nights scrolling through Facebook, laughing and joking and never getting real. I pretended we'd let ourselves go, been honest, that we'd told each other everything. The character who emerged seemed Dan-like, true to Dan, more Dan than Dan had ever been. So much so, it was an entirely new person, and that made me feel like my possession of his memory, *our memory*, was complete somehow.

I wrote a thirteen-thousand-and seventy-six-word story. I tried to paste it onto my Facebook page, but it wouldn't stick. Too much language for the afterlife, I suppose. WTF.

Tarot
by Diana Salas-Deitch

the Artist, Diana Salas-Deitch
by Nicholas Deitch

196

THE ALCHEMY OF OBSERVATION

A CONVERSATION WITH DIANA SALAS-DEITCH

by Calla Gold

In the world of art, there are those who paint what they see, and those who paint what the light suggests. For Diana Salas-Deitch, the artist behind the visual landscape of our current issue, the process is a lifelong experiencing of the world. From the interlocking squiggly lines she drew as a seven-year-old to the sophisticated, translucent washes of her current watercolors, Diana's journey has been defined by a refusal to stay inside the lines.

Roots in Resourcefulness

Diana's creative origin story is a beautiful blend of domestic ingenuity and international exploration. She remembers her mother—a military spouse raising four children—who fashioned hand-drawn figures into paper patterns to sew clothes from scratch. "My mom taught and modeled how to be resourceful and creative," Diana reflects, noting that those fabric remnants were the early seeds of her own love for textile and fabric arts.

This foundational creativity was refined further in the third grade while Diana was living in Japan. Under the guidance of a teacher who encouraged students to study a tree branch with all five senses, she'd feel every crease of the bark and view the unique lines and study how the varying directions, patterns, and colors were affected by light.

"My teacher gave me permission to think outside of the box and assured me that there was no 'right' or 'wrong' in creating art," she said. "To this day, I enjoy 'Happy Accidents' in my work—it's all good."

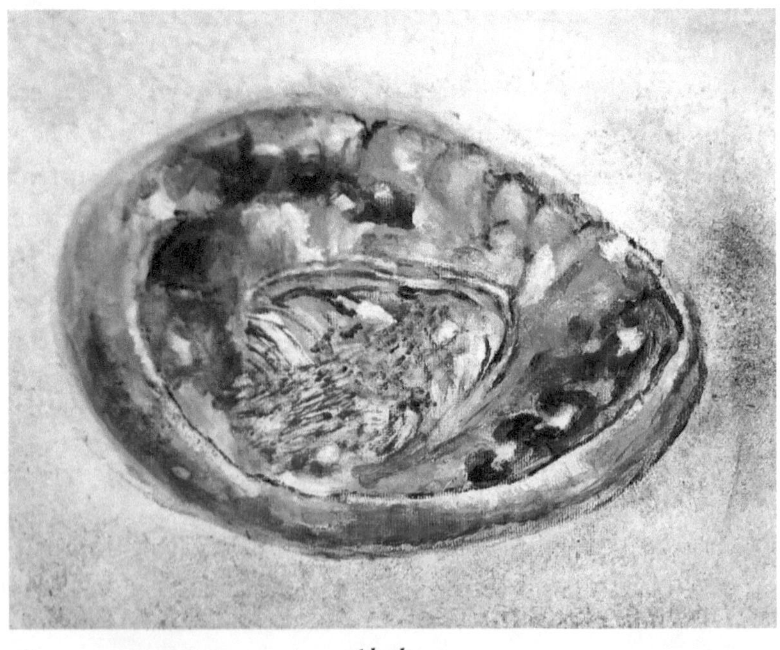

Abalone
by Diana Salas-Deitch

The Science of Light and Mood

When discussing her technique, Diana speaks of light as if it were a living character. She isn't just looking at a face; she is watching how a skylight elevates a person's features into a mystical or dreamlike look. "I am often fascinated by the many ways light influences my perception of what I actually see," she said.

Her artistic heroes reflect this obsession with form and color: the simple still lifes of Cezanne, the tropical vibrance of Gauguin, and the boundary-pushing collages of Picasso and Matisse. Like them, Diana balances the tactile—having once dominated her living room with a massive floor loom for weaving—with the fluid, currently rediscovering the transparent beauty of watercolor.

Creating Art for *Mysterious Ways*

Tasked with interpreting the theme of *Mysterious Ways* for this volume, Diana did more than just illustrate, she became an immersive reader. "I percolated ideas," she explained. "I immediately immersed my energy into reading the selected fiction works...re-reading the stories snumerous times."

Her sketches became a silent dialogue with our authors. Whether it was being transported by the character of Ashara in Alyson MacInnis's *Kept,* or researching the high-stakes environment of an interstellar spaceship for Jeremy Gold's *The Recycler,* Diana sought to capture the spark of each piece. For the story *The Girl Who Wrote the Storm,* she even found herself reading aloud in a Gaelic-ish accent to better feel the rhythm of the prose before picking up her brush.

"I love it when writing is rich with inferences and connections, as well as when it leaves room for my imagination. I've found these elements in much of the writings selected for this latest edition."

A Shared Creative Life

This deep respect for the written word likely stems from Diana's own life; she is married to a writer, Nicholas, whose 18-year journey to finish his epic novel has been a shared adventure. She describes herself as his greatest fan, a role that mirrors her broader commitment to the arts community—from donating work to local causes to participating in the Ventura ArtWalk.

Ultimately, Diana's advice to anyone dabbling in the arts is the same mantra she gives herself: "Have fun exploring and experiencing art in its many forms." For this issue, that exploration has resulted in a collection that doesn't just sit alongside the stories—it breathes with them.

Woman in Doorway
by Diana Salas-Deitch

THE [UN]USUAL SUSPECTS
our contributors

Kunal Basu is an author of fiction and poetry. His 11 novels and 2 volumes of short stories have been published worldwide, translated into many languages and adapted for cinema. His poetry has appeared in *Parnassus, Riverrun, Interface, The Telegraph* and *London Magazine*. He teaches at the University of Oxford.

Christopher Buckley's *SPREZZATURA* is published by Lynx House Press, 2025. His work was selected for Best American Poetry 2021 and he is the recipient of a Guggenheim Fellowship in Poetry, two NEA grants, a Fulbright Award in Creative Writing, and four Pushcart Prizes. One Sky to the Next, was winner of the Longleaf Press book Prize for 2022. Christopher is a local Santa Barbara writer who attended Mt. Carmel school and Bishop High, and taught at UCSB College of Creative Studies. He lives on the mesa.

Jenny Burman has an MFA in fiction from the Iowa Writers' Workshop (1998). She's been published in *Tin House, Black Clock, The LA Weekly, Los Angeles Magazine, Cincinnati Magazine, Akashik Mondays Are Murder* and other publications.

B.J. Burton, writer of short stories, plays, poetry, and nonfiction, has had work published in *The Orchards Poetry Journal, Philadelphia Poets, Philly Fiction,* and elsewhere. As a produced and published playwright, her plays have been seen by audiences in Philadelphia, Pittsburgh, and New York. Honors include two Fellowships from Pennsylvania Council on the Arts. She received her MFA at Rosemont College, where she was on the faculty for several years.
https://www.linkedin.com/in/b-j-burton-055062a9/

Eugene Datta is the author of the poetry collection *Water & Wave* (Redhawk, 2024) and the story collection *The Color of Noon* (Serving House Books, 2024), which has won the first Walter Cummins Short Fiction Book Award. His work has appeared widely both online and in print, with some having been anthologized, and translated into German, French, Arabic, and Italian. Nominated for a Pushcart Prize and the Touchstone Award for *Individual Haibun*, he lives in Aachen, Germany.

Nicholas Deitch is a writer, architect, and advocate for social justice whose fiction explores the intersection of cities, history, and human resilience. He has honed his craft, publishing short stories in *Litro Magazine, Club Plum, Santa Barbara Literary Journal,* and *The Southern California Writers Association Anthology of Short Stories.* His short story *Grace Eternal* won Best Fiction at the Santa Barbara Writers Conference (2019). His novel, *Death and Life in the City of Dreams* (Acorn Publishing, April, 2026), is a multi-generational work of literary eco-fiction exploring the life and tribulations of an American city across 150 years. Originally from Los Angeles, Nicholas now lives in Ventura, California, with his wife and creative partner Diana.

William Doreski lives in Peterborough, New Hampshire. He has taught at several colleges and universities. His most recent book of poetry is *Cloud Mountain* (2024). He has published three critical studies, including *Robert Lowell's Shifting Colors.* His essays, poetry, fiction, and reviews have appeared in various journals.

Chynna Foster is a clinical psychologist and poet based on the South Coast of Australia. Her work explores memory, embodiment, grief and the legacies we inherit. Chynna is currently working on her first collection.

Valerie Girard has practiced holistic health for over forty years. She has also explored the art world as a theater director, playwright, composer, musician, poet, oil painter, photographer, and published author. Currently, she is finishing her third nonfiction book. She has contributed articles to magazines, sharing her insights on health and spirituality. Valerie teaches meditation and yoga and feels a strong connection to the mystery of life and its valuable lessons. Additionally, she has created and uploaded more than 350 meditation videos on her YouTube channel, @QuantumWhisperer.

Calla Gold is an editor as well as a contributor. You can read Calla's bio on page 212.

Jeremy Gold has published one novel, *Death in Carp High,* and has been published in several previous editions of *Santa Barbara Literary Journal.* He enjoys the retired life in Carpinteria, California, with his wife and fellow writer, Calla Gold.

Khris Golder recently placed as a finalist in *Santa Clara Review's* Flash Takes Flight literary contest. He has other published nonfiction (*202 Magazine, Discover the Phoenix Region*), poetry (*Wingless Dreamer, The Raven's Muse*), and fiction (*The Horror Zine, Beyond Words, Wicked Shadow Press*). Born in San Jose, he lives in Phoenix with his wife and son.

Samantha Grabler is an author from New Jersey who has spent much of her formal career researching cancer and autoimmune diseases. Outside of lab life, Samantha enjoys nature and developing her writing. Originally intended to process trauma, her poetry has grown into a relatable, explorative wrangling of the ineffable. She focuses mostly on the human experience, nature, and spirituality, often with scientific undertones.

Stella Ho is a writer and market research analyst from the Bay Area. Her work is featured or forthcoming in *Berkeley Poetry*

Review, Westwind Journal of the Arts, October Hill Magazine, Eucalyptus Lit, Berkeley Fiction Review, and elsewhere.

Christine Jackson has contributed to several educational journals and is the principal editor of *Provocations*, an on-line journal for arts educators. For years, she has written poetry and short stories without seeking an audience. After 30 years as a passionate arts and literacy educator, Christine now turns her attention to the craft of writing. This is her second publication of poetry. Christine lives in Toronto.

Juyanne James is a Louisiana native and is the author of *The Persimmon Trail and Other Stories* (Chin Music Press, 2015), as well as *Table Scraps and Other Essays* (Resource Publishers, 2019). Her stories and essays have been published in journals, such as *The Louisville Review, Bayou Magazine, Eleven Eleven, Thrice, Ponder Review, Xavier Review, Burningword Literary Journal*, and *NonBinary Review*, and included in the anthologies *New Stories from the South: 2009* (Algonquin) and *Something in the Water: 20 Louisiana Stories* (Portals Press, 2011). Juyanne lives and teaches in New Orleans.

Naomi Bess Leimsider's poetry book, *Wild Evolution*, was published by Cathexis Northwest Press in June 2023. In addition, she has a poetry chapbook forthcoming from Finishing Line Press in Winter 2026. She has published poems, flash fiction, and short stories in *Branches, Ellipsis, Lothlorien Poetry Journal, Midway Journal, Heavy Feather Review, Mantis, Unleash Lit, Packingtown Review, Tangled Locks Journal, The Avenue Journal, Booth, Anti-Heroin Chic, Wild Roof Journal, Planisphere Quarterly, Little Somethings Press, Syncopation Literary Journal, On the Seawall, St. Katherine Review, Exquisite Pandemic, Orca, Hamilton Stone Review, Rogue Agent Journal, Coffin Bell Journal, Hole in the Head Review, Newtown Literary,*

Otis Nebula, Quarterly West, The Adirondack Review, Summerset Review, Blood Lotus Journal, Pindeldyboz, 13 Warriors, Slow Trains, Zone 3, Drunkenboat, and *The Brooklyn Review.* She has been a finalist for the Acacia Fiction Prize, the Saguaro Poetry Prize, and the Tiny Fork Chapbook Contest. In 2022, she received a Pushcart Prize nomination for fiction.

Nathan Loceff was born and raised in Santa Rosa, California. His first collection of poetry and short fiction, *Joys of the Capital,* came out in 2016. His work has been published in *3:am Magazine, Belleville Park Pages, Scrawl* and elsewhere. He lives in Paris and his creative writing project exploring the Eiffel Tower can be found at: theeiffeltoweris.wordpress.com

Alyson MacInnis is a writer who lived another life first, bringing a seasoned eye for atmosphere and human contradiction to her essays and short fiction. She writes from Southern California. Find her work on Substack at *Among the Running Horses* amongtherunninghorses.substack.com.

Wendy Jean MacLean's work is shaped by her lifelong engagement with mythology, gospel and spirituality. Her award-winning poetry has been published in over thirty journals, including *Presence, Kosmos, Crosswinds, Amethyst Review, Streetlight* and commissioned and performed by outstanding choirs internationally.

Zach Keali'i Murphy is a Hawaii-born writer with a background in cinema. His stories appear in *Raritan Quarterly, Reed Magazine, The MacGuffin, The Coachella Review, Another Chicago Magazine, The Vassar Review, FOLIO,* and more. He has published the chapbook *Tiny Universes* (Selcouth Station Press). He lives with his wonderful wife, Kelly, in St. Paul, Minnesota.

Shira Musicant writes short fiction and creative nonfiction and has received four Pushcart Prize nominations. Her work has been previously published in *Santa Barbara Literary Journal* and can also be found in *Fourth Genre, SmokeLong Quarterly, Bending Genres, Milk Candy Review* and other literary journals. Recently retired from her practice as a somatic psychotherapist, Shira lives in Santa Barbara with her husband, a black cat, and eight chickens. shiramusicant.com

Ted Olson is a 2019 MFA graduate of the Rainier Writing Workshop at Pacific Lutheran University. After working 31 years as a copywriter, he's pursuing his love of fiction and creative nonfiction. Ted's work has appeared in *The Write Launch, Griffel,* and *Half and One.*

Mona Leigh Rose's stories appear or are forthcoming in *TriQuarterly, Pinch, Santa Monica Review, Summerset Review,* and *Puerto Del Sol,* among others. She is an Associate Fiction Editor at *Narrative Magazine,* and is honored that one of her stories appears in the flash fiction anthology *The Best Small Fictions* guest edited by Amy Hempel. She lives and writes in Santa Barbara, California.

Eddi Salado is a California based poet and retired educator. She studied Creative Writing at College of Creative Studies, UCSB. Her work has appeared in *Spectrum, Feminist Studies, Gunpowder Press,* and other publications. A selection of her poems were used in a song cycle entitled *Blood Poems,* and performed in Lisbon, Portugal. She is a member of CPITS, California Poets in the schools.

Diana Salas-Deitch is a Ventura-based artist whose work explores the intersection of light, memory, and nature. From her early years in Japan to her decades of watercolor practice, Diana's art is defined by what she calls "happy accidents" and a deep, multi-sensory observation of the world. She is a frequent participant in the Ventura ArtWalk and a passionate advocate for arts education in local schools. For Volume 13, Diana immersed herself in our fiction selections to create a visual dialogue that captures the "mysterious ways" of our shared human experience. Read more about Diana on page 197.

B. Geren Sanford crafts richly textured worlds, filled with unforgettable characters, while steeped in science and lifted by the fantastical. Professionally, as Brian Grant, he designs engaging learning experiences and advocates, in articles and presentations, for the power of using stories and world-building in training and development. He also produces music under the moniker Vox Humanic and in the collaborative band DETLAS. Learn more: bgerensanford.com, voxhumanic.com, and detlas.com

Terry Sanville lives in San Luis Obispo, California with his artist-poet wife (his in-house editor) and two plump cats (his in-house critics). He writes full time, producing stories, essays, and novels. His stories have been accepted more than 600 times by journals, magazines, and anthologies including *Folio, Bryant Literary Review,* and *Shenandoah.* He was nominated four times for Pushcart Prizes and once for inclusion in *Best of the Net* anthology. Terry is a retired urban planner and an accomplished jazz and blues guitarist – who once played with a symphony orchestra backing up jazz legend George Shearing.

Peter Schwartz is a poet, artist and musician. Also, a few other things including a deli clerk, but the point is you should go to https://the-art-of-peter-schwartz.jimdosite.com.

Michael Spivack is a lifelong composer of sound and language, who works cycles between the measured and the intuitive, from studio monitors to morning meditations, from voice systems to verse. He's spent recent years shaping dialogue in the world of conversational AI, designing the tone and cadence of machines that speak, while privately returning to the blank page where nothing has to make sense but everything must feel true. With a background in music production and storytelling across records, film, and product design, Michael approaches poetry much like he approaches sound: as an architecture of silence and resonance. His work explores presence, fatherhood, spiritual inquiry, and the search for steadiness in a world built on noise.

Caitlin Swalec is a wild swimmer and trail runner based in Santa Barbara, California. During adventures in the ocean and mountains, she often reaches a meditative flow state that helps her process her anxiety and fears, mainly stimulated by climate change advocacy, her chosen profession. She uses this creative state to craft poetry as a form of expression to reflect on her experiences in this world, including her athletic endeavors like swimming the Santa Barbara Channel in 2023 and running the Grand Canyon Rim to Rim to Rim (R2R2R) last fall.

Veronica Tucker is an emergency medicine and addiction medicine physician, mother of three, and lifelong New Englander. Her writing explores the intersections of medicine, motherhood, and the human experience. A Pushcart Prize nominee, her work appears in *ONE ART, The Berlin Literary Review, Rust & Moth,* and elsewhere. Her chapbook *The House as Witness* is forthcoming from Quillkeepers Press. veronicatuckerwrites.com Instagram: @veronicatuckerwrites

Tom Tulloh is a poet and translator, living in a French post-industrial port that frequently overwhelms his senses. His translations of Arthur Rimbaud have been published in *Noria revue.* In addition, his translation of the short story, *The Sofa* by Jean-Luc Raharimana appeared in *Your Impossible Voice.* Most recently, Tom translated Franck Gourdien's poems, *Who goes there* and *March into a monster* for *ANMLY*.

Reed Venrick resides in France part of each year and writes on French history, culture, and language.

Kirby Michael Wright was born and raised in Hawaii. His family land on Moloka'i served as the breadbasket for Kamehameha's warriors while training for their assault on Oahu.

Woman at Blinds
by Diana Salas-Deitch

THE EDITORIAL TEAM
who we are

Maryanne Knight, Editor-in-Chief
Maryanne joined the editorial team in 2021, stepping into the role of Editor-in-Chief with the publication of Volume 12.

She loves stories that follow unexpected paths and poems that deepen in meaning with each subsequent reading. As editor, she is eager to promote new writers of any age and to publish a wide array of voices from around the world.

Maryanne's short stories have appeared in *Santa Barbara Literary Journal, On the Run, Grand Dame Literary Journal, The Yard (Crime Blog)*, and the anthology *The Fifth Fedora.* MaryanneKnight.com.

Zachary Murdock, Poetry Editor
• Musician, Poet, Creative Director
• Host of The Pink Hearse Podcast
• Founder of Channel the Sun

Nose in a novel. Raising a child. Humming Sly and the Family Stone. Writing pre-dawn poetry. Cooking. Cleaning. Exercising. Rinse and repeat. My daily life is simple. And this routine allows me to be the farmer of an overflowing dream vineyard.

Poetry into songs, songs into visions, visions into webs of community and collaboration. I live and breathe creativity in all forms and am grateful to be navigating reality on a trippy Quixote steed in the form of a pink hearse with hubcap mirrors.

Calla Gold, Fiction Editor

Calla owned a jewelry design business for thirty-eight years. Her Indie non-fiction book *Design Your Dream Wedding Rings, From Engagement to Eternity*, was released on Valentine's Day 2019.

Her recent short stories and novelette have been published in *Mobius Blvd, Killer Nashville Magazine,* and *Confetti Magazine.*

Calla resides in southern California with her husband and an assortment of mountain bikes.

Fred Williams, Fiction Editor

Fred brings readers a new storytelling experience guiding them down a twisted rabbit hole where moral ambiguity abounds. Fred has been featured in *Santa Barbara Literary Journal,* and had one of his tales published in Max Talley's *Delirium Corridor.* He also released his first novel, *Scramble: The Perfect Recipe of Math, Murder, and Revenge* in 2020 to critical acclaim. www.fredcreates.com.

Junior Bases, Assistant Editor

Junior is an aspiring author, editor, and adult. Currently in his last year studying English and anthropology, Junior helps edit fiction and runs the blog for *Santa Barbara Literary Journal.* Creatively, he has a fiction story published in Volume 11, and more journalistic pieces published across other sites. His writing style is short, bare, and emotional, often exploring growth, separation, and family.

Max Talley's new detective thriller, involving extortion and sex trafficking in New Mexico, arrives in local bookstores, on Amazon, and at Lazarusmedia.net in May 2026.

Santa Barbara Literary Journal
www.santabarbaraliteraryjournal.org

Volume 1: *Andromeda*, June 2018
Volume 2: *Cor Serpentis*, December 2018
Volume 3: *Bellatrix*, June 2019
Volume 4: *Stardust*, November 2019
Volume 5: *Wild Mercury*, September 2020
Volume 6: *Saturn's Return*, June 2021
Volume 7: *Oh, Fortuna!*, August 2021
Volume 8: *Moon Drunk*, December 2022
Volume 9: *Space Sirens*, June 2023
Volume 10: *Satellite of Love*, January 2024
Volume 11: *This Must Be the Place*, November 2024
Volume 12: *Superposition*, September 2025
Volume 13: *Mysterious Ways*, May 2026
Coming Soon!
Volume 14: *Liminal Spaces | The Noleta Issue*, November 2026

Other Collections
Hurricanes & Swan Songs, April 2019
Dames & Doppelgangers, October 2019
Delirium Corridor, December 2020
Silver Webb's All Hallows' Eve:
The Thinning Veil, October 2021
The Fifth Fedora, Fall 2022
A Flash of Darkness, April 2023
When the Night Breathes Electric, September 2023
Dragons of Aeronoth, February 2024

ACCEPTING SUBMISSIONS NOW

Lazarus Media Publications LLC

133 E De la Guerra, #161
Santa Barbara, CA 93101

info@lazarusmedia.net

(805) 729-2969

www.ingramcontent.com/pod-product-compliance
Lightning Source LLC
Chambersburg PA
CBHW032235050726

47591CB00001B/400